# MY MISTLETOE MIX-UP

## A RIDGEWATER HIGH NOVELLA

# My Mistletoe Mix-Up

## JUDY CORRY

Copyright © 2018 by Judy Corry

**ISBN:** 978-1-957862-08-8

All rights reserved.

This is a work of fiction. Names, characters, organizations, places, events, and incidents are either products of the author's imagination or are used fictitiously. Any resemblance to actual persons, living or dead, or actual events is purely coincidental. No part of this book may be reproduced in any form or by any electronic or mechanical means, including information storage and retrieval systems, without written permission from the author, except for the use of brief quotations in a book review.

Cover Illustration by Wastoki

Edited by Precy Larkins

Also By Judy Corry

**Ridgewater High Series:**

When We Began (Cassie and Liam)

Meet Me There (Ashlyn and Luke)

Don't Forget Me (Eliana and Jess)

It Was Always You (Lexi and Noah)

My Second Chance (Juliette and Easton)

My Mistletoe Mix-Up (Raven and Logan)

Forever Yours (Alyssa and Jace)

**Eden Falls Academy Series:**

The Charade (Ava and Carter)

The Facade (Cambrielle and Mack)

The Ruse (Elyse and Asher)

The Confidant (Scarlett and Hunter)

The Confession (Kiara and Nash)

**Standalone YA**

Protect My Heart (Emma and Arie)

Kissing The Boy Next Door (Lauren and Wes)

**Rich and Famous Series:**

Assisting My Brother's Best Friend (Kate and Drew)

Hollywood and Ivy (Ivy and Justin)

Her Football Star Ex (Emerson and Vincent)

Friend Zone to End Zone (Arianna and Cole)

Stolen Kisses from a Rock Star (Maya and Landon)

*For my wonderful readers*

## PLAYLIST

"Perfect" - One Direction
"Girls Like You" - Walk off the Earth
"Melodies of Christmas" - David Archuleta
"Home This Christmas" - Justin Bieber feat. The Band Perry

## CHAPTER ONE

"SORRY NOAH TURNED you down at the game," my best friend, Alyssa, said as she parked her Honda a few houses down from her boyfriend Trey's house. "Do you still think you'll be able to get a date before the Christmas Ball?"

I sighed and unbuckled my seat belt. "I have no idea. I wouldn't know who to ask." I'd stuck all my eggs in the Noah-Taylor basket and now I was running out of time to find a date.

Why had I been so stupid to think that just because we'd made out at one party meant he might actually like me?

"Don't worry, Raven. I bet there'll be plenty of guys at the party tonight willing to go with you."

*Willing to go.* That wasn't romantic. I wanted this to

be the year I finally had a boyfriend to take to the annual Cheerleader Christmas Ball. A guy who I was excited to go with and who was excited to go with me.

Call me a hopeless romantic, but I dreamed of the day a tall, dark, and handsome guy would want me for more than just a night of non-committal kissing. I wanted a boyfriend. I wanted what Alyssa had with Trey. One of those relationships that everyone envied.

Yes, I knew I didn't *need* a guy. But I wanted one.

I sighed and climbed out of Alyssa's car. She joined me on the sidewalk a second later, and we walked up the hill past the houses lit with colorful Christmas lights. Trey's house, also known as "Party Central," was at the end of the cul-de-sac.

"I think I saw that trumpet player, Harrison, checking you out during the game," Alyssa said, her breath visible in the cold December night air. "I heard he just broke up with his girlfriend, too."

I made a face. Harrison was a band nerd. Sure, I liked music as much as the next girl...but he just wasn't my type. I wanted the type of guy that walked into a room and stole everyone's attention. A guy that you couldn't help but take a second look at and stare at for a few seconds.

There had to be a guy like that somewhere, right?

"We need new guys at our school," I finally said. That was the only option left.

Alyssa laughed. "Or maybe you need to stop being so picky."

I rolled my eyes. "Says the girl who already has the perfect boyfriend."

Alyssa just shrugged. "I'll tell Trey you wish he had a twin."

I smiled. "Yeah, you go tell him to make that happen." Trey wasn't exactly what I'd call a hottie, but he was cute in a boyish sort of way. And him and Alyssa looked good together.

When we were one house away, Alyssa pulled her phone out of her back pocket. "I'll text Trey, so he knows we're here. It's probably a madhouse in there."

"As usual."

Trey was on the basketball team, and since they'd just won tonight's game they were bound to be in a celebrating mood.

We climbed up the front steps and were about to knock when the door opened wide and Trey filled it. "Welcome to the party." Trey pushed his strawberry-blond hair out of his blue eyes.

Alyssa gave Trey a quick hug and a kiss before walking in.

Once the door was shut behind us, Trey looked at

Alyssa with excitement in his eyes. "I have a surprise for you out back."

She furrowed her brow. "You do?"

He nodded. "Yeah. But we need to hurry before he gets too cold."

"He?" Alyssa and I both said at the same time.

Trey grinned. "Yes, *he*." Then he took Alyssa's hand in his and tugged. "Come on. You're going to be shocked."

Alyssa turned back to me with her eyebrows raised. "I guess I'll be back in a while. Will you be okay on your own?"

I scanned the room. It was full of cheerleaders and jocks. "Pretty sure I'll be fine." These were my people.

I weaved my way through the living room until I found my other friends from the cheer squad, Megan and Rachel.

"Hey, Raven." Megan gave me a quick side hug. "I didn't know if you were coming tonight."

I tucked some of my long, black hair behind my ear. "Uh, yeah. I had a last-minute change of plans."

"Oh yeah, I kind of saw that," Megan said.

Of course, pretty much the whole school saw me get shut down...again.

I turned to Rachel, hoping she'd have something interesting to say so we wouldn't have to keep talking about my guy failures.

"Did you hear the Carmichael twins moved back to Ridgewater?" Rachel asked, her eyes bright with excitement.

"What?" My jaw dropped. Jace and Logan were back? In Ridgewater? "Who told you they're back?" I quickly glanced around the room to see if they were here.

"I totally saw Jace in the kitchen a few minutes ago."

My heart raced at the prospect of Jace being here at the party. Would he remember me?

He'd better remember me. We'd been next-door neighbors all growing up.

Megan looked at us both with a confused expression. "Am I supposed to know who the Carmichael twins are?"

How could she not know who the Carmichael twins were? They were legendary around here.

"They're only the hottest guys to ever walk the earth," Rachel said, matter-of-factly. "It's like God knew he'd made a masterpiece, and so he couldn't help but make two of them."

"So they're hot?" she asked.

"Do you really not remember them?" Rachel furrowed her brow, confused.

"No," Megan said.

It was then I realized why Megan wouldn't know who they were.

"Of course she doesn't remember them," I said to

Rachel. "They moved away right before Megan moved here."

Understanding washed over Rachel's face. "Oh. That's right."

Rachel launched into an explanation about how the Carmichael twins had moved away to North Carolina the summer after our freshman year. As she spoke, I scanned the crowd for their familiar faces. If they were really back, that would be amazing.

Memories of all the times I'd watched Jace and Logan play basketball in their driveway next door popped into my head. I'd been ridiculously in love with Jace all through middle school and freshman year. He and Logan were identical twins. The only reason people had been able to tell them apart was because Jace actually combed his hair, whereas Logan seemed like he just ran a hand through his and called it good—and despite my preference for the put-together look, there were many girls who had fallen for Logan's more tousled, bad-boy style.

But not me and Alyssa. We'd been obsessed with Jace all through middle school, always trying to get a peek at him through his bedroom window, which was across from mine, whenever we had sleepovers.

Which was why I'd never gotten the courage to tell him that I liked him. Alyssa and I had both agreed that he would have to be the one to pick between us without us making the first move. That was the only way things would be fair.

But now she was dating Trey, so...

Maybe this was the universe's way of telling me it was time to take a chance. Maybe Noah had to totally turn me down at the basketball game tonight, so I could be open to something with Jace.

"Do you think Jace is still in the kitchen?" I asked Rachel once she'd finished giving Megan the details about the twins.

Rachel shrugged. "He could be."

My hands felt sweaty at the thought.

"Is Logan here, too?" I asked.

Rachel shrugged. "When I asked Jace, he said Logan had decided to stay home to read a book."

"Logan wanted to read a book?"

Rachel gave me a look that told me she was just as surprised as I was. "That's just what Jace said."

Weird.

"I'm going to go grab a drink from the kitchen," I said.

Rachel gave me a knowing grin. "I bet you are."

So it was totally obvious that I was going looking for Jace. Oh well.

I walked into the kitchen but didn't see Jace, just a few basketball players with big red cups, laughing about something in a corner.

That was the one bad thing about partying with the basketball team. They were all about getting drunk on the weekends and didn't realize that some of us wanted to actually remember what we did at parties.

I settled for water from the tap then went to the dimly lit dining room in the back to see if I could spot Alyssa and Trey in the backyard. He had to have shown her his surprise by now.

I peeked through the blinds in the door but didn't see anyone.

I blew out a long breath and turned around. I almost dropped my cup when I saw that I wasn't alone in the dining room. Just a couple of feet away was a guy who looked familiar, but also different. He was a few inches taller than he'd been the last time I'd seen him. His hair was cut in the new trendy way, which looked amazing on him. His shoulders were broader. His jaw more defined.

I'd thought he was drop-dead gorgeous when we were fifteen, but time had definitely been good to him. Jace Carmichael was possibly the most beautiful guy I'd ever seen.

I cleared my throat to get his attention. And when he slowly pulled his gaze away from the window to look at me, my blood completely froze up. Wow. Just, wow. His eyes were as steel-blue as ever.

"Hi," I managed to gasp out as my pulse skyrocketed.

Jace's lips curled up into an easy smile. "Hi."

I sucked in a deep breath through my nose, hoping it would calm me so I wouldn't act like a total fangirl.

"Rachel said she ran into you here. When did you guys get back?" I asked. *Act cool. Don't go all gaga over him.*

But who was I kidding?

He was real.

He was here.

Hopefully he was single, too.

He took a sip from his water bottle. If I'd had any doubt about who I was talking to before, aside from the fact that his hair was actually combed, that water bottle was my clue. Logan had always been the first to suggest raiding his parents' wine cabinet. Jace had been the one with the water bottle to make it clear that he wasn't drinking.

Jace screwed the cap back on his bottle. "We just got here today."

"And you guys are back for good? Not just visiting your grandma for Christmas?"

"Yep, we're back for good."

I bit my lip to try to keep from grinning at the thought of having Jace at school with us again.

"Did you miss me, Raven?" Jace asked, a teasing grin on his face.

Wow, I was being so obvious.

But I couldn't help it. I'd had such a crappy time at the game tonight and seeing Jace again after all this time was too good.

"I guess I sort of missed you."

"Yeah?" He raised his eyebrow and inched closer. "But do you even know which twin you're talking to right now?"

"Yes..." I said it slowly, not quite as confident as I'd been a moment before.

"So which one am I then? Logan or Jace?"

"You're Jace, of course."

His grin stretched broader. "And what makes you think that?"

Well, honestly, it was because Rachel had told me that Jace was at the party and Logan was at home reading a book.

But I wouldn't tell him that. This was my chance to let Jace know just how much I had noticed about him. I knew that the twins had always wanted to be set apart from each other—wanted their own identity. Which was why they had created their own looks. Jace was the clean-cut twin who you could depend on. Logan was the goof-off who was always getting into trouble.

"I know you're Jace, because firstly, you're holding that water bottle instead of a cup filled with beer. Secondly, I haven't heard of anyone getting into a fight yet tonight, and we all know how Logan could never resist starting one. And third, your hair is a dead giveaway. You actually took time to comb it instead of running your hand through it and calling it good like Logan does."

His grin broadened as I finished my list. "I had no idea you were so perceptive, Raven."

I shrugged. "It's a gift. I like to call it my sixth sense."

He stepped closer. "Did your sixth sense clue you in to what we're standing under right now?"

What?

I tipped my head back to see what he was talking about. And to my surprise, I was standing right beneath a sprig of mistletoe. The evergreen shrub with white berries was practically mocking me with how close it was to the door.

My cheeks flushed. "I promise I didn't know that was there."

He gave me a knowing smile. "You sure you weren't planning to give me a special welcome back to Ridgewater?"

My cheeks burned hotter. "I—"

He stepped closer. "Because it seems awfully wasteful not to use this moment. I think the universe might be trying to tell us something." He winked.

"It is?" I managed to say. Was this actually happening?

He stepped even closer until we were only inches apart. He reached his hand forward and twisted some of my hair around his finger. "I've always wanted to do this." The low tone of his voice turned my insides to mush.

Jace Carmichael was touching my hair! "Y-you have?"

He nodded, and his steel-blue eyes bore into mine. "You have to know that I've always had a crush on you, right?"

My heart stuttered in my chest. Was I dreaming? Was Jace Carmichael, the guy I'd crushed on for years, actually telling me that he had secretly crushed on me, too?

I was speechless. I pinched myself to see if I was really awake.

Jace's gaze dipped down to where I'd just pinched myself. "This isn't a dream, Raven."

Gah. What was I supposed to do?

Usually, I was so much better with guys. I had always prided myself on how easily I flirted. I could go up to a random guy at a party and know for sure that he'd happily make out with me. I'd gotten the nickname "Rebound Raven" for a reason.

But this was different. Because this was Jace. This was the guy who had moved away, who I thought I'd never see again.

He let my hair untwist from his finger and looked up

at the mistletoe above our heads again. "So, what do you say, Raven? Want to give it a chance?"

Okay, I needed to get my crap together. I could *not* miss this once-in-a-lifetime opportunity.

And I needed to do it with dignity, too. If I was too scared to kiss him, there was no way the kiss would be any good. I needed to be there for it. I needed to be confident.

I needed Jace to think he was lucky to have a chance to kiss me.

"Do you think you can handle a kiss from me?" I asked, forcing as much confidence into my voice as I could.

"Oh, I think I can." He raised his eyebrows in a challenge.

"You sure? Because I know you haven't been here for a while, but my kissing skills are pretty much legendary."

"Legendary? That's a big word."

My mind was telling me to back off. That I was pushing things too far.

But I wanted him to expect to be amazed, because if he had that expectation, it was more likely to happen.

So I moved even closer until there was no space left between us. I tilted my head up to look at his handsome face. "If it seems like it's the wrong word for this moment, maybe you should help me figure out a better one," I whispered. And when our eyes met, I saw something spark in his.

He really did want to kiss me.

"I'm pretty good with big words." He bent his head close to mine, and his fingers slipped across my neck until he was cradling my head.

My eyes fluttered shut as I became overwhelmed with being so close to Jace. A second later, his warm, minty breath caressed my lips, causing chills to race across my skin. And then his mouth was on mine. I went still, not actually expecting him to follow through with the kiss, but then we fell into an easy rhythm.

I let my hand slip up his chest and neck until it rested against his jaw. His jaw was strong. I'd always wondered what he'd look like once he hit his growth spurt, but my imagination hadn't done him justice. He was a work of art.

I slowly ran my thumb across his jawline as heat swirled in my veins. I had always loved kissing—loved the feeling of being close to a guy I was attracted to. I loved to forget about all the pressures of life. Loved to just live in the moment with someone else, exchanging something we both enjoyed.

But none of those kisses had been like this. Kissing had always been my favorite distraction, but as our lips got to know each other, I couldn't help but think kissing Jace might just be the best distraction of all. I never thought a tiny sprig of mistletoe could change a person's life. But this small moment with Jace just might have the chance to alter mine forever.

The kiss lasted for less than a minute, but when we pulled away from each other, I couldn't keep a huge grin from my face.

I licked my lips, committing his peppermint Chapstick to memory. He tasted like a candy cane. "I think I need to thank Trey's mom for hanging the mistletoe right here," I said, letting my bravery stay a moment longer.

"I should thank her, too." He pressed his lips together as if he was trying to savor the taste of my lips on his for a moment longer as well.

Had I really just kissed Jace Carmichael?

I was about to suggest that we test the mistletoe again when the door beside us suddenly opened, making me jump.

Jace and I stepped away from the door to allow who ever had opened it to come inside. A second later, Alyssa and Trey walked in holding hands, and behind them was a guy who looked exactly like Jace.

Had Logan started combing his hair?

And why would Logan be with Alyssa and Trey? *Jace* had been Trey's best friend before they moved. Not Logan.

"Oh, hi, guys," Alyssa said when she saw me and Jace.

"Hi," I said, my voice sounding confused.

"We were just coming to show you my surprise," Trey said. "But it looks like you already figured it out."

"Yeah, Jace and I were just reacquainting ourselves with one another," I managed to say, hoping they couldn't read on my face that we'd just been kissing.

I really hoped Alyssa wouldn't be mad at me. We'd always said we'd let Jace decide. He'd been the one to point out the mistletoe...so I had kind of stayed with the plan.

Plus, she was dating Trey, so she shouldn't care, anyway. But when Alyssa furrowed her brow at me, I worried that maybe she was upset.

She pointed to the twin who had come in with them. "But this is Jace."

"Hi, Raven." The Carmichael twin who just came inside waved to me. "Long time, no see."

"Hi...?" I turned back to the guy I'd just been kissing. "Logan?"

A smirk spread across his face, and he took my hand in his and shook it. "It was a pleasure to run into you again, Raven."

I just stood there, completely dumbfounded. Had I just kissed Logan?

His smirk got bigger when he saw the confusion on my face and he leaned in close to whisper in my ear. "You might want to get that sixth sense of yours checked. It was way off." Then he stepped back and spoke loud enough for everyone to hear, "It was great to see you all again. But if you'll excuse me, I have somewhere else to be."

And before my brain could wrap around everything that had just happened, that jerk raked his fingers through his hair a few times to loosen his locks until they looked tousled. Then he opened the back door and left the party.

## CHAPTER TWO

I COULDN'T STOP TOUCHING my lips the rest of the night after I found out that I'd kissed Logan Carmichael.

*Logan!*

And I hated that in the moment I had liked it. You'd think that my body wouldn't have reacted so positively to that lying jerkface. But apparently, my body was just as big of a traitor as he was.

Oh well. I'd be prepared the next time I saw him.

I woke at eight the next morning, since I had a Christmas charity event to get to. My mom had noticed me being kind of "bah humbug," as she liked to say, and had signed me up to help at this Winter Wonderland thing where less fortunate kids would sit on Santa's lap and tell them what they wanted for Christmas.

I wasn't excited, but since it was my mom and I loved her, I tried to not be too pessimistic about it.

When I got to the community center at nine-thirty, the woman in charge, Elizabeth, handed me a green dress with red petticoats poking out from the bottom. "You're going to be one of Santa's helpers. I think this should be about your size."

I took the dress into the makeshift changing room that they had set up in the back and got changed. When I looked in the mirror, I couldn't help but think that the people in charge of this thing actually had decent taste in costumes. I wouldn't necessarily wear this elf dress with the candy cane striped socks to a party, but it wasn't too bad.

When I walked out of the changing room, I almost bumped right into someone.

"Oh, sorry," I said as I jumped back. And when I looked up, I was met with a familiar face.

I gasped. "Jace?"

And then he took off his baseball hat to reveal his messy hair. "It's Logan." He smirked and put the hat back on. "Man, Raven, that's two strikes in a row."

I rolled my eyes and set my clothes on the counter beside me. "Sorry, *Logan*. I guess it's just the wishful thinking part of my brain kicking in."

He laughed. "You know you're happy to see me again."

I shook my head. "You wish." Then I noticed that he was holding an elf suit in his hands.

"Are you helping here, too?"

He shrugged. "I had to catch up on my community service hours from before we moved away."

"Seriously?"

He smirked. "No. I'm just doing this out of the kindness of my heart."

"You have a heart in that beefy chest of yours?"

He put his hand over where his heart should be. "Your words cut me like a knife, Raven."

"At least I don't go around kissing people, pretending to be my brother."

He raised his eyebrows in a suggestive way. "But at least when I do, I make it worth their time. You can't tell me you didn't like it."

It took all my facial muscles to try to keep a smile off my face. "So, you've had a lot of practice. You better be good at kissing with as much as you do."

"So you think I'm a good kisser, then?" He leaned closer with a flirtatious smile on his lips.

I folded my arms. "You were fine."

"Just fine?" He cocked an eyebrow. "From how pink your cheeks are, I'd say I was better than fine."

I rolled my eyes again and gestured at his costume. "You better put that on. The kids will be here any minute."

He didn't immediately go into the changing room. Instead, he just looked at the red shirt, candy cane striped suspenders, and green shorts with a look of disbelief. "When Elizabeth called this morning to ask if I could help out, she didn't tell me I'd be wearing the costume I wore when I was twelve."

"You've done this before?"

"Remember what I said about all that community service?" he asked.

"I thought you were joking?" Logan was the bad boy. The guy who cared about no one but himself. He wasn't the kind of guy who would willingly help out less fortunate kids on the weekends.

"My dad had me and Jace doing this thing ever since fifth grade. Elizabeth was practically frantic when the new kid called in sick this morning. So, since Elizabeth is a sweetheart, I told her I'd come."

"Are you sure you're Logan? Because the Logan I know doesn't call people *sweethearts*."

He stepped closer to the changing room. "Maybe you don't know me as well as you think."

---

"YOU COMING OUT SOMETIME TODAY?" I called to Logan after he'd been in the changing room for ten minutes.

"Not unless there's a fire," he said, his voice void of all enthusiasm.

"Come on. It can't be that bad," I said. And if it was, I totally wanted a picture of it. "The kids are almost here. You're going to have to come out sometime, you know."

He groaned. "How good are you at lying?"

I scrunched up my face. "What?"

"How good are you at lying?" he repeated.

Was it possible that he really did look terrible in the costume? I'd never seen the Carmichael twins look bad in anything, but maybe the universe was giving back some of the karma Logan deserved.

"I'm not nearly as good at lying as you are." My mom and dad usually had to tell me that being completely honest in my opinion of things wasn't always the best way to make friends.

"Then I think I'm going to just live here now."

I shook my head. It couldn't be that bad. And since I was pretty sure that he was fully dressed, I opened the curtain myself.

I had to cover my mouth to stifle a huge laugh. The costume did *not* fit him. At all. The red shirt was stretched so tight across his torso—if he flexed just right, he would probably burst out of it like the Hulk. And the green shorts only hit him about mid-thigh.

Logan scowled at me. "Tell me I look good."

I couldn't help myself. I had to laugh.

"Are you sure they got your size right?" I asked between giggles.

He shook his head. "Apparently, Elizabeth didn't realize that I'd gained about six inches in the last year and a half."

I stepped in the changing room to get a better look. "It's not so bad," I lied.

He glanced down at himself. "These green shorts and suspenders look like lederhosen. People should not be seeing this much of my leg."

I smiled, but I had to agree. They were pretty much an elfed-up version of lederhosen. But instead of totally making fun of him and giving him the payback he deserved for his trickery last night, I said, "You have nice legs."

He scoffed. "You were right, you're a horrible liar."

I shrugged. "Sorry. But I'm sure it'll be fine. Just put on the cute elf hat and pointy ears and no one will be looking at your legs." I pointed to the accessories on the plastic chair behind him.

He just stared at the green hat and ears. "Just pretend like you think I'm Jace, okay?"

"Sorry, you have hat hair. I can't just make my brain

switch when it knows that Logan has messy hair and Jace doesn't."

He took off his hat and smoothed his hair with his fingers until it resembled how it'd been last night under the mistletoe. "Better?"

"Nope. Now you're just making me wonder if you're trying to trick me again like you did last night."

But *daaaang*. He looked fine with his hair tousled, but when it was combed like that...he really did look just like his brother.

And when he looked like *that*, I couldn't help but remember how I'd kissed him last night.

He caught me staring at him. "What?"

"Um, nothing." I shook my head before I could imagine what it would be like to kiss him again.

Would I like it as much if I knew it was Logan?

"From the expression on your face, I'm guessing that you think I look worse like this?"

"Yes."

His expression fell as he checked his reflection in the mirror. "Worse for sure?"

I stepped forward and slipped my fingers into his hair to mess it up a little, trying not to notice how soft his hair was. "I didn't mean that. I just meant that I think the tousled hair helps with the elf look."

And it helped me to stop daydreaming about our kiss,

when I'd thought he was Jace. As long as Logan kept his hair this way, I could stop fantasizing about kissing Jace.

Yes, Jace. Not Logan. Because why would I ever fantasize about kissing Logan? We hated each other.

He turned toward the mirror and coifed his hair until it was tousled just the right way above his gorgeous face.

Not that I thought Logan was gorgeous.

Jace was the gorgeous one.

Even if they looked the same.

*Okay, Raven. Stop thinking stupid thoughts.* Logan was bound to notice how frazzled he was making me.

I drew in a deep breath and focused on my mantra. Logan was annoying. Logan was a jerkface. Logan was the worst.

I would just keep chanting that in my head until my brain remembered it believed it.

He studied his reflection in the mirror for a moment longer, and I was thankful he didn't seem to realize how attracted I was to him right now.

Then he turned back to me and shrugged. "I guess this is as good as it's gonna get."

## CHAPTER THREE

WHEN LOGAN and I made it back to the Winter Wonderland scene, Elizabeth handed me a clipboard. Santa was already sitting in his over-stuffed red chair. There were a few adults making last-minute touches to the fireplace scene—adding a few ornaments on the Christmas tree behind Santa and duct-taping the stockings that just didn't want to stay up firmly to the cardboard fireplace.

"If you could just write down the names of the children as they sit on Santa's lap and write down what presents they ask him to bring in the column next to their name, that would be perfect."

I looked over the sheets attached to the clipboard. There was space for fifty children. We were going to be busy for a while.

Elizabeth turned to Logan next, who I still couldn't look at without snickering at his outfit. "If you could help the smaller children get onto Santa's lap and then back down afterward, that's all we'll need you to do."

He swallowed and looked around before saying, "I don't know if I'll be able to bend over very far to get the little ones."

Elizabeth gave him a confused look. "Are you injured?"

He shook his head and cleared his throat. "No, um." He looked around again before lowering his voice to just above a whisper. "I don't know if you noticed, but this costume is just a bit tight this year, and if you don't want me to split my shorts in front of all those innocent children's eyes, I might need to be careful with my movements."

Elizabeth's eyes widened as she took him in. It was like she was actually seeing him for the first time since we'd left the back room. She cleared her throat. "My dear. You *have* grown. This doesn't fit you at all."

Logan shook his head. "Nope."

Elizabeth chewed on her lip as she tried to figure out what to do. Then she glanced at her watch. "The families should be here any minute. There isn't time for us to see if we have an alternative costume somewhere in storage."

"I'm not saying I need to change," Logan said. "Just

trying to warn you what might happen if I bend over too far."

She looked at his shorts, and I couldn't avoid letting my gaze wander to his backside as she did. Yep, he was definitely crammed in there tight. If only I hadn't left my phone in the other room, I could have totally snapped a photo and sent it around as blackmail for what he'd done to me last night.

"How about we have you two switch spots," Elizabeth said, breaking me away from my revengeful thoughts. "Logan can take notes and Raven can help the children. Does that sound okay?"

I thought about saying that no, it wouldn't work out because I really wanted to have a good laugh at a possible wardrobe malfunction from Logan. But I decided to be nice instead. "Yeah. That works."

I handed Logan the clipboard and he mouthed, "Thank you."

"I might need you to write my mom a letter telling her that I've become a model citizen and have a heart of gold after this, okay?" I said to Logan as we walked onto the small stage where everything was set up.

"As long as you don't take any pictures to use for blackmail, I'll write anything you want."

It was like Logan could read my mind.

"TEN MORE KIDS and we'll be done," Logan spoke in a quiet voice when I came to stand by him. A cute three-year-old girl was sitting on Santa's lap, telling him that she wanted something pink for Christmas.

"Too bad," I said to Logan. Surprisingly, this helping-people-out thing was fun. Who knew helping bring joy to others could be fulfilling?

"You're just sad because you don't want to return that cute dress," he said.

"Oh, so you think it's cute?" I asked with a flirtatious tone before I remembered that I didn't flirt with Logan

"Yep. Pretty sure that's what I'd ask Santa to bring me for Christmas."

He smiled, totally flirting back, so I decided to take it as a compliment. "I'll make sure to whisper it in Santa's ear for you."

"Speaking of Santa..." He gestured at the little girl who now had her hands on Santa's face as she told him exactly all the pink things she wanted. "That little girl is just all sorts of adorable."

Did Logan just say the word *adorable*?

I looked at the girl. Her blonde hair was pulled up into curly pigtails with pink bows, and she was dressed in pink from head to toe. Even her snow boots were pink.

The girl spoke in her soft three-year-old voice, "I want a pink doll. Pink clothes. Pink backpack. Pink shoes..."

"Are you getting all that?" I asked Logan, eyeing his clipboard.

"Ah, yes." He quickly lifted the clipboard in his arm and started scribbling down notes.

"You forgot the pink unicorn," I whispered, and when I leaned in closer I caught a whiff of his delicious cologne.

He added *unicorn,* and in big letters above all the words, he wrote "Pink" with arrows pointing at everything.

I watched the crowd as the little girl went on and on. There were a few girls about our age huddled together with goofy grins on their faces. And they were all watching Logan.

"Don't look now, but I think you have some admirers in the crowd." I leaned closer to Logan as he continued scribbling the little girl's list.

His pen stilled. "Admirers?" He gave me a confused expression.

I pointed to the three girls who must go to the other high school in Ridgewater. "They're totally checking you out."

"In this ugly thing?" He made a face. "What's wrong with them?"

I laughed. "Maybe they have a thing for elves in tiny costumes."

He shook his head. "And maybe they need to have their heads examined."

I couldn't help but laugh. And when the tall red-headed girl in the middle winked at him, I laughed again.

"Please tell me she didn't just wink at me," Logan said.

"She totally did." I grinned. "I think she likes your costume. A lot."

Logan glared at me. "You seriously need to work on your lying, Raven. You suck at it."

"I'll take that as a compliment."

While Logan was trying to avoid the gazes and the little waves from his admirers in the back, I noticed that the little girl had finally finished her very detailed list of things she wanted for Christmas. So I helped her down from Santa's lap and held her hand as she descended the steps toward her father at the bottom of the stage.

I bent down so I was closer to the little girl's eye level. "Now make sure you be extra sweet and kind to your family, and I'm sure Santa will be able to do something about getting you your pink Christmas."

The little girl beamed up at me and said, "I be extra good."

I grinned back at her and patted the top of her head. "That's good to hear."

She ran over to her dad and threw herself into his

open arms as she excitedly told him about all the things she asked Santa for.

When I made it back to the front of the line, I found that Logan had decided to take my duty over for me.

He handed me the clipboard as he carried a baby boy who couldn't be more than a few months old. "You take the notes. I'll take care of the kids. I gotta move around so I can turn my back to those girls. They're starting to weird me out."

I took the clipboard into my hand, resting it against my arm. "You know they're just going to be watching you from behind, right?"

He groaned. "Yeah, but at least I won't have to see it."

He carefully carried the baby over to Santa and set him on his lap. The baby instantly burst into tears and reached for Logan. And my heart kind of wanted to melt a little as I watched Logan pick the baby up again and gently bounce him to calm him down. The baby stopped crying, but instead of putting the baby back on Santa's lap, Logan knelt beside Santa's chair and held him close to Santa, so his parents could snap a photo.

Once the photo was taken, Logan carefully cradled the baby in his arms and carried him back to his young mother.

And as I watched the whole exchange, I couldn't help but think that Logan was surprisingly good with kids.

Who woulda thought the bad boy was a big softy?

## CHAPTER FOUR

"I THINK I just got my man card back," Logan said as he hung his costume on the rack. His baseball hat was back on his head and he wore his t-shirt and jeans that fit him just right.

I hung my costume next to his. "You didn't look that bad. I mean, at least those girls in the back didn't think you looked bad."

He rolled his eyes. "You're going to milk that for as long as you can, aren't you?"

I smiled and pulled on my red coat. "Let's just say it's slightly satisfying to have you be the embarrassed one for once."

"Well, I guess if it helped all those kids have a better day, then me losing all of my dignity was worth it." He shrugged his coat over his broad shoulders and zipped it up.

I started to call my mom and tell her I was ready to be picked up. One of these days I'd get my own car.

Logan must've realized what I was doing, because he asked, "Are you calling someone for a ride? Because I can just drop you off somewhere if you want."

I looked down at my phone, contemplating whether I trusted Logan behind the wheel or not. "How many accidents have you caused this year?" I asked.

He scrunched up his face. "What?"

I shrugged. "Before I accept your offer, I need to know how much of a risk I'm taking if I get in a car with you." You could never be too careful. Especially with someone like Logan behind the wheel.

He scoffed. "I haven't gotten in any accidents since I got my license. I'm actually a pretty good driver, Raven."

"You sure about that?" I asked skeptically. "I seem to remember that time freshman year when you stole your dad's car and drove it into a pole."

He ran a hand through his hair and actually looked embarrassed. "Okay, so I used to be a little irresponsible back in the day. But I've taken driver's ed since then, and I don't have any alcohol in my system like I did that time, so you're completely safe."

"You were drinking that day?"

His eyes got a pained look in them. "I did a lot of

stupid things back then. But I promise I don't drink anymore. It might have taken me a while, but I did finally learn my lesson."

I peered into his eyes carefully, like I'd be able to tell if he was telling the truth or not. Then I held up my hand with my pinky finger extended toward him. "Pinky swear?"

He stared at it for a moment before locking his with mine. "Pinky swear."

I pulled my hand away from his, trying to ignore the zing of electricity that I felt as our skin touched.

I pushed my hands into the front pockets of my coat. "My mom's probably still in the middle of her DAR Christmas banquet anyway, so I guess I'll let you take me home."

Logan chuckled. "I like how you turned it around to make it seem like you're doing *me* the favor by allowing me to transport Her Majesty home." There was a lightness in his voice as he twirled his key ring around his finger.

I stood taller and tossed some of my hair behind my shoulder. "Well, I am pretty important around here."

I had expected him to come up with some sort of jab, but surprisingly he didn't. He just said, "I'm out this way," and led me toward the back exit.

When we walked into the parking lot, there were only a few cars left: a silver Ford about ten years old, a white

Tahoe, and a fancy black Corvette that definitely looked out of place.

I headed toward the Ford, assuming that it must be Logan's car.

He didn't follow me. When I glanced back, he nodded toward the Corvette. "Uh, I'm parked over there."

"That's yours?" My jaw dropped. Logan drove a Corvette?

"Yeah, my mom kind of went overboard for me and Jace's sixteenth birthday," he said sheepishly.

I just stared at the shiny black car and tried to calculate in my mind how much a car like that would cost.

What had happened when they moved to North Carolina? Because the Carmichael family that I grew up next to did not have the kind of money to buy their son a car like that.

"Does Jace have a Corvette, too?" I couldn't help but ask.

He shook his head. "No. He got a Tesla."

I just stood there stunned over the fact that their mom had spent more on their birthday presents combined than my parents had probably bought our house for.

My legs finally decided to work again, so I followed Logan to his car. "So I'm guessing moving to North Carolina turned out to be an okay thing for your family?"

Logan got an embarrassed look on his face. "Yeah, I

guess you could say that." He rubbed the back of his neck with his hand. "So, do you still want a ride?"

"Do I still want a ride?" I asked, still not believing that he had a Corvette. "Of course I want a ride. There's no way you're leaving this parking lot without me in that car."

"So you're okay with the Corvette?" he asked.

Was he really thinking I'd turn down a ride from him because his car was too fancy? "I've always wanted to ride in a Corvette, Logan. So, yeah. I'm okay with it."

He looked relieved.

"Do people usually turn you down for rides?" I had to ask as he opened the car door for me.

He shrugged. "Sometimes. But that's usually because they prefer Jace's Tesla."

"Well, those people are just crazy."

"Wait." Logan touched my shoulder, stopping me before I could climb into his car. "Did you just say that someone would be crazy to pick Jace over me?"

I laughed. "No. I just said picking a Tesla over a Corvette is a bad choice."

He pursed his lips. "Too bad. I thought you might actually be coming to your senses, because it's obvious that I'm the far superior twin."

"Says the guy who was pretending to be his brother last night."

He scowled. "That was different. We were just testing everyone to see if they could tell us apart."

"And did anyone pass?"

"Nope. Not even the girl who used to spy on us as we played basketball in our driveway."

My jaw dropped. "You saw me?"

He grinned. "Yep. Pretty much every time."

My cheeks heated. "Does Jace know?"

He shook his head. "No. I was nice and kept it our little secret." He winked, and I wanted to slap that smirk off his face. Logan was so conceited sometimes.

But instead of giving in to my urge, I climbed into his car. It was surprisingly warm inside, and I realized that he must have turned it on with his key as we'd walked over.

I buckled myself into the black leather seat and just looked around the dashboard as Logan walked around to the driver's side. I'd never been in a car half this fancy.

And a teenager drove this?

What had happened when they moved to North Carolina?

Logan turned to me after he buckled himself in. "Do you still live in the same house?"

"Yep."

"Cool. I haven't seen our old house since we moved. This gives me an excuse to drive by it."

"So what did your parents do for work when you

moved to North Carolina anyway?" I asked when he turned onto the road.

Logan shifted down as he turned a corner. "My dad finally decided to join the Carmichael family business again."

That must be some family business if they could buy cars like this after only a year and a half. They hadn't been poor before they moved, but they most definitely hadn't been rich like this, either.

"Why did you guys move back here, anyway?" I asked.

"My mom missed New York and my dad got to where he could work remotely, so it just seemed like the right time. We liked Sweet Water, but it wasn't home, you know."

I nodded, watching the snow-covered trees as we drove down the quiet road. "I love Ridgewater."

We pulled onto Elm Street a minute later. "Your mom's still obsessed with Christmas, isn't she?" Logan commented when my house came into view.

It was my mom's goal every year to have the house with the most lights. I'd loved it when I was a kid, but now it was just kind of embarrassing.

Logan pulled up to the curb. "I guess I'll see you at school on Monday?"

I unbuckled and pulled on the door handle. "Yep. Thanks for the ride."

I climbed out, but before I could shut the door, Logan leaned over the passenger seat. "What? No goodbye kiss like last night?"

I rolled my eyes. "In your dreams, Logan."

"Always," he said with a wink, just before I closed the door.

## CHAPTER FIVE

I WAS DOODLING in my notebook early Monday morning before school started when someone sat in the desk in front of mine and said, "Miss me?"

I looked up to find Logan. He wore a long-sleeved navy-blue shirt and jeans, and I couldn't help but notice how the blue of his shirt really brought out his eyes.

But what was he doing in Honor's English? Mrs. Reynolds was super picky about who they allowed in this class. And Logan was far from the model student.

At least the Logan I knew from before hadn't cared about his grades.

"Are you sure you're in the right class?" I asked him. "You're not just stalking me, right?"

A slow grin spread across his lips. "This is Honor's English, correct?"

I nodded. "Yes."

"Then this is exactly where I'm supposed to be. Are you surprised Mrs. Reynolds let me in?"

"Yes, actually. You're about the last person I expected to see in an honors class."

"I'm not an idiot, you know." His smile faltered momentarily, but he smoothed it back onto his face. "You have to be smart to get into as much trouble as I used to get in."

I laughed. "Used to get in? Meaning, you don't get into trouble anymore?"

He shrugged and put his notebook on his desk. "I'm a work in progress."

I nodded. "That's what I thought."

I pulled out my English binder and the book we were reading as a class, *The Crucible*, and set them on my desk.

Logan turned to face the front of the class and I watched the back of his head as we waited for the bell to ring. He had a nicely shaped head, and I had stared at one just like it many times over the years.

Would Jace be in any of my classes today?

"Did you happen to tell Jace about our misunderstanding Friday night?" I whispered to Logan.

He turned back to me. "*Our* misunderstanding? I think you mean *your* misunderstanding. I knew exactly who I was the whole time."

I rolled my eyes. "Okay, fine. *My* misunderstanding."

He tapped his pencil against the edge of the desk. "I didn't want to embarrass you with how obsessed you still are with my brother, so I didn't tell him."

"I'm not obsessed with him."

He raised his eyebrow. "Really?"

I shifted uncomfortably in my chair. "No. I was just excited to see him again. Or excited to see who I thought was him."

He leaned closer. "Well, I hope I didn't disappoint you too much."

My face flashed with heat as he just looked at me for a moment. It was like he was trying to figure out how my thoughts about him differed from my thoughts about his brother.

"I wasn't that disappointed," I said after a beat. "Mostly just surprised."

His gaze went down to my lips for a moment. Then he said, "Good."

I was still trying to figure out what he meant by "good" when Emily James walked up to me. "Hey, Raven."

"Hey." Emily was on the cheer squad with me. Her mom was the one in charge of this year's Christmas Ball. And while we were teammates, we weren't exactly best friends.

She ran her hand along the shoulder strap of her backpack. "Were you able to get a date for next Saturday?"

Ugh. Why did she have to come ask me that when Logan was right there?

I gritted my teeth. "I'm still working on it."

She gave me a fake smile. "I thought I heard something like that. I heard Noah turned you down at the game on Friday. So sorry to hear."

Yeah, she sure sounded sorry. But I managed to put as fake of a smile on my face as she had. "I was just asking him to hang out as a friend."

"Well, that's a relief. Since I guess you heard he and Lexi got back together this weekend, anyway."

I furrowed my brow. "They did?"

"Yep." She nodded. "Anyway, my mom is trying to get a count of who's going to be at the ball with dates, so she knows how much food to order and how many tables to set up. So, just make sure to let us know soon. And as you remember from last year, there's always room at the singles table if you can't get a date." She gave me a condescending pat on the shoulder.

My body tensed with her touch, but I forced myself not to show how much she was getting to me. "Okay, thanks, Emily."

Then thankfully, she continued to her desk at the back of the room.

I turned back to my notebook and started doodling my signature along the lined paper, so I wouldn't have to think about how embarrassing it was that Logan had just overheard that conversation.

But since Logan couldn't just let me be humiliated in peace, he swiveled around in his chair and said, "So, you tried to replace your crush on my brother with Noah Taylor?"

I pressed my pen harder against my notebook as I finished writing the "S" in my last name. "You know it's not nice to eavesdrop, right?"

"Good thing I wasn't eavesdropping then. Just overhearing."

I sighed. "You caught me. I liked Noah Taylor." But was that really that big of a surprise? Pretty much every girl I knew had a thing for Noah.

"That's surprising."

"Why would that be so surprising?"

He shrugged. "I never expected you to like someone like him."

"And why's that?"

"Probably because you've always liked my brother."

"And that means I could only ever like someone like Jace?" I asked.

He shook his head. "No, it's just that Jace is way different. He doesn't have a bad bone in his body."

He was right. Jace was very different from Noah. "Every girl has a soft spot for a brooding bad boy."

He raised his eyebrows. "I don't believe you. You can't tell me that if you were given the choice, you'd choose me over my play-it-safe brother." The intenseness of his stare made my skin prickle with heat.

Did he really think the only reason why I liked Jace more than him was because Jace was the safe choice?

Had he forgotten all the times he'd teased me growing up? Had he forgotten about tricking me on Friday night?

Sure he'd been nice enough on Saturday at the Winter Wonderland thing, but that didn't automatically cancel out everything he'd done in the past.

"My preference for Jace isn't just because he's safe. It's because he's actually nice to girls."

Logan crossed his arms. "I can be nice."

I raised an eyebrow in a challenge. "Yeah, but for how long?"

"As long as I want."

I shook my head and smiled. There was no way Logan could be nice. I knew I wasn't exactly the kindest person all the time, but at least I could pretend when I wanted.

He must have seen my doubts on my face because he said, "I've just never had a reason to want to be nice to you before."

The room started to get noisier as more students

walked in. I looked at the clock above the whiteboard. The bell would ring in less than a minute.

"So you're saying that you could be a perfect gentleman to me if you wanted?"

"Yeah, it'd be easy."

"For more than a few hours?"

"Do you really think that badly of me?"

I shrugged. "I'm just skeptical. History has proven otherwise."

"Fine. You need a date for the dance, right?"

"Yeah..." I said the word slowly.

"Let me show you just how nice I can be and let me take you to the Christmas Ball."

He was asking me to the dance?

"Why would I want to go to a dance with you?"

"Because you don't want to give Emily the satisfaction of seeing you sit at the singles table again."

It *would* be nice to actually show up with a date. And while Logan wasn't Jace, he was just as hot. Even with his bad-boy look.

Plus, there had been quite a few of the girls in the cheer squad posting in our group messages over the weekend about the Carmichael twins being back in town and how they wanted to be the ones to finally tame Logan.

"What's in it for you?" I asked.

"I get to have the satisfaction of proving you wrong," he said.

It wasn't exactly the romantic offer I'd been hoping for. But if it helped me save face, make a bunch of my friends jealous, and teach Logan a lesson at the same time, maybe it wouldn't be such a bad thing.

"Okay, fine. I'd love to go to the Christmas Ball with you."

For a second, he looked like he thought I was joking, but when I didn't add a "just kidding" at the end of my sentence, he said, "Then it's a date."

"Really? Just like that?" I asked.

He shrugged. "As long as you promise not to fall in love with me, then let's say I'll pick you up next Saturday at seven, okay?"

I scoffed and crossed my arms. "I don't think there'll be a problem with any feelings getting involved."

"Good. Because while I know I'm quite the catch, I just got out of something and don't need you trying to find ways to sneak any mistletoe into the dance." He shot me a conceited grin.

I resisted the urge to roll my eyes. "I'll make sure to ask Mrs. James to keep the mistletoe locked up."

"Perfect."

The bell rang, and Logan turned around just as Mrs. Reynolds walked to the front of the class. And as she pulled out her copy of *The Crucible* from the pile on her desk I couldn't help but think that it was such a coincidence in a way. Of course I would end up going to the dance with a guy who just got out of a relationship. That was how it always went.

But thankfully this time, there was no risk of me actually falling for Logan. Of that, at least, I was sure.

## CHAPTER SIX

ENGLISH ENDED up being the only class that I had with Logan, thankfully. But apparently, that was the only nice thing the school secretary had done for me, because Jace, sadly, wasn't in any of my classes. I barely even saw him at school.

Alyssa, on the other hand, got to sit right next to him during U.S. History. But she told me that he mostly just took his notes quietly, so she said I wasn't missing much, really.

"It's like he's mad at me or something," Alyssa said to me Friday as we warmed up before the boys' basketball game. "Trey says he's been acting weird around him, too. It makes me wonder if Jace and Logan switched personalities when they moved to North Carolina because Logan has been way nicer to me than he used to be."

I finished my round of jumping jacks and sat on the dance lab's wood floor to stretch. "You think Logan's nice?"

Alyssa sat across from me. We put our feet together, clasped our hands, and she pulled me closer to her to give my hamstrings a good stretch. "I didn't say he was nice, just nicer." She shrugged. "But he does seem different than he used to be. He doesn't seem as mad at the world, anyway."

I thought about it. We had talked a few times in English class this week and he'd been unusually pleasant. I'd assumed he was just getting a head start on practicing being nice to me at the dance next Saturday, but maybe it was more than that.

Was it possible that Logan had really figured out how to be kind?

We finished our warm-up a few minutes later and grabbed our pompoms so we could head across the hall to the gym.

Alyssa and I were just walking through the door when Logan stopped me. "Hey, can I talk to you for a minute?"

I looked at the scoreboard. The game was set to start in twenty minutes. There were already a bunch of fans and students in the bleachers, watching the varsity team warm up on the floor.

"Okay."

He pulled me back into the hall where it was quieter. "Did you get your dress for the dance yet?"

"Yeah, why?" As soon as my mom found out I was going with a guy instead of by myself, she'd taken me shopping that very afternoon.

"I was gonna go shopping tomorrow to find a tie that matches."

"Oh," I said, surprised that Logan would even think about that kind of thing. He seemed like the kind of guy who would tell a girl that he was wearing what he wanted and getting all matchy-matchy took away his freedom of expression.

At least that was what the old Logan would do.

"So what color is your dress?"

"It's white and pink." It had a white lace-embellished bodice and a full pink skirt to be exact, but I doubted Logan cared about those details. He was a guy, after all.

"Pink?" he frowned. "Did you pick pink just so I'd be forced to wear a pink tie?"

I laughed. "No, I actually wasn't thinking about you when I picked it. I picked it because I look good in it."

He raised his eyebrow. "Oh, you do?"

I felt myself blush. "Yes."

"Lucky me."

And I don't know why I hadn't put it together before,

but I suddenly realized that Logan and I were going to a dance together. Which meant, I'd have to dance with him.

Butterflies erupted in my stomach at the thought.

But I urged the butterflies to go back to sleep. I shouldn't be excited to dance with Logan.

When I didn't say anything, he asked, "Could you send me a picture, so I don't pick the wrong tie?"

"And ruin the surprise when you pick me up?" Wasn't there some sort of rule about that?

Wait no, that was just weddings. And Logan and I were about the last people on earth who would ever wind up married someday.

"Well, you don't want me to get a shade of pink that clashes, do you?"

"No."

"You could always just send a pic of a part of the skirt."

I nodded. "Okay." When I started to walk back to the gym, he touched my shoulder to stop me. I turned around. "What?"

He cleared his throat. "You forgot to get my number."

I furrowed my brow. "Why would I need your phone number?"

"So you can text me the photo."

"Oh." Realization dawned on me. "Well, my phone is in my cheer bag, so I don't have it with me."

He pulled his phone out of his pocket. "Here, just put your number in mine and I can text you my number."

I transferred my pompoms into my left hand and took his phone. When I pushed the button, a photo of a mountain with the words "One day at a time" showed up on the lock screen.

Logan's gaze instantly flicked to his lit-up screen. "Sorry, I must not have unlocked it." He quickly took it back as if embarrassed that I'd seen the quote. He handed it back a second later, and I found his contacts and added my name and number.

"Just don't send me any weird texts." I handed his phone back to him.

"You wish."

---

I WAS WORKING on my U.S. History homework the next morning when my phone buzzed with a text.

Logan: **I know you wanted to keep your dress a secret but while our personalities already clash, I don't think our formal wear needs to.**

I put my hand to my head. I'd completely forgotten to send him a photo of my dress last night. So I went to my closet to take a picture of the fabric really quick.

I pressed on the photo and uploaded it in a message with the words, "**here you go.**"

I set my phone face down on my desk so I could get back to my homework. It buzzed a second later.

Logan: **I'm not very good at matching clothes. Do you want to just help me pick the tie?**

What?

Logan: **Please.**

Since when did Logan learn to say please?

And why did he want to spend time with me?

I looked at my planner. I didn't have any other homework besides this one. I guess I had the time.

Plus, it would only make us look bad in front of the whole cheer squad if our outfits clashed next weekend.

So I texted him back.

Me: **Let me eat some lunch and then I can go.**

Logan: **Do you like Cafe Amore?**

I furrowed my brow. Why did he want to know that?

Me: **Never been there. Why?**

Logan: **I was planning to eat there. It's right next to the place where my dad used to get his suits. We can eat then shop.**

Was Logan asking me on a lunch date?

I shook my head. It was best if I didn't try to figure him out. That boy was just confusing.

But since I loved eating out and trying new foods, I went against my better judgement and texted him back.

**Sounds good.**

---

LOGAN PICKED me up in his Corvette thirty minutes later. He looked like he'd just showered, and I couldn't help but notice how good he smelled when I sat in his car. He didn't look so bad, either. But I figured that when you were a Carmichael, you'd actually have to *try* to look bad to make it happen.

He pulled onto the road and started heading toward the center of town.

"Is that a different hat?" I asked after giving him an inspection and noticing his blue New York Yankees baseball hat. He'd worn a green one last week.

He ran a hand over it. "Yeah, this is my out-on-the-town hat." His smirk told me he was joking, and it was funny to think about him accessorizing his hats based on what he was doing each day.

"Does that mean you have hats for other occasions?"

He nodded. "Of course. There's my studying-for-a-test

hat. My going-to-pick-up-a-girl hat. My hiding-from-the-paparazzi hat."

"You're joking, right?"

He took his focus off the road to glance at me. "Mostly joking."

"So does that mean you're not just being even lazier about your hair?"

"Me lazy? Never." He winked, and my heart did a little blip in my chest.

Strange.

"Okay, so then what is that blue hat for again?"

He shrugged. "It's my 'show Raven Rodgers that I can actually be a nice guy' hat."

I laughed. "And does it work?"

"I guess we'll find out by the end of the afternoon, won't we?"

He pulled into one of the shopping malls a few minutes later and parked. Logan led me toward a shop with the sign "Cafe Amore" above it.

The bell on the door jingled as we walked into Cafe Amore.

I couldn't believe I'd never noticed this place before. From the outside it looked a little run-down, but when we walked inside, the ambiance was really nice.

There was a Christmas tree in one corner and a garland lining the front counter. Twinkling lights were draped across the high ceiling, which added a super cozy feeling to the room.

"I've been craving this place since we moved to Sweet Water. Have you really never eaten here?" Logan asked as we got in line to order our food.

"Nope."

He gave me a puzzled expression, like he was trying to figure out if I'd lived in some alternate version of Ridgewater all these years, but he didn't say anything about it. Instead, he said, "Well, the menu is just up there." He pointed to the wall behind the cashier that had printed white papers stapled to a cork board. "It's not the fanciest place, but as long as it hasn't changed too much since I've been gone, whatever they lack in atmosphere they make up for with the actual food."

"I'll let the food speak for itself." I scanned the menu. "So what's the best thing they have here?"

His gaze ran over the menu as if trying to figure out which of the dishes I might like. Then he shrugged. "I really like the Italian club sandwich with the pub salad."

I wrinkled my nose. "I don't feel like a sandwich or a salad. Do they have pasta?"

"Yeah." He looked around the wall for a moment before pointing to the right side. "The pasta choices are there."

I pressed my lips together and checked the list. Three-cheese penne, fettuccine Alfredo, and the classic lasagna among other choices. "Is there a certain dish you'd recommend?"

He eyed the menu again before turning to me with a bashful look on his face. "Now that I think about it, I've only ever ordered the Italian club sandwich and the pub salad when I've been here."

"This is your favorite restaurant and yet you've only tried one thing on the menu?" Now it was my turn to look at him like he was an alien. "That's ridiculous! You know that, right?"

He shrugged his broad shoulders. "I guess I found something that I liked and decided I was happy with it."

"You're funny, Logan." To think I thought he was a bad boy all these years. If he wasn't daring enough to try new foods, how bad could he even be? "Think you want to try something new today?"

He shook his head. "Nope, I'm good with the regular. I haven't been here in a year and a half, so I think it's okay if I get something that I know I'm going to like."

I folded my arms and turned back to the menu. "To think all these years I thought you were the adventurous twin."

He pouted. "I am adventurous. I mean, I'm taking you to a dance next week. What's more adventurous than that?"

"Getting that redhead's number last week would have been the real adventurous thing to do."

"Ha-ha, Raven. You're soooo funny." Then he said, "Fine. You want me to prove to you how adventurous I am?"

I nodded, my interest piqued at what he was going to suggest. "Yes."

"I'll let you choose my order for me."

"You trust me to order your food?" I raised my eyebrows, surprised. "You *are* brave."

He lifted a shoulder. "Just don't tell them to add any poison to it, okay?" He held a fifty-dollar bill out to me. "And so I'm not tempted to commandeer the order, I'll go find us a table and be surprised when the waitress brings it."

I looked at the money. He carried fifty-dollar bills with him? I understood tens, and twenties, but fifties?

I took the money. "Any drink requests?"

He took a step back. "Surprise me."

"Okay."

Then a thought seemed to occur to him. "But promise you aren't going to purposely order me something nasty, okay?" He held up a pinky. I shook my head but linked pinkies with him, anyway.

"I promise. It will be something that I think sounds good, at least."

He smiled, glancing down at our hands for a moment. Then he raised his gaze back to mine and there was something in his eyes that hadn't been there before.

Could he feel something every time we did that, too?

I let my hand drop back to my side before I could think too much about it. "I'll come find you in a minute."

## CHAPTER SEVEN

I WATCHED Logan carefully as he took the first few bites of his lunch. I had ordered him a French dip sandwich and a berry salad with pecans and feta cheese. It'd been risky to order him a salad, since guys my age seemed to think salads were for girls. But he'd said he normally ordered the pub salad when he came here, so I'd figured it might be okay.

"So what's the verdict?" I asked.

He set his fork down on his plate. "Do you really want to know?"

I tried to gauge what he thought from the look on his face but couldn't get a good read. So I slipped my most confident smile onto my face. "I'm actually expecting to hear that this is the best meal you've ever had, ordered for you by the most intuitive person you've ever met."

He laughed. "You really do believe in that sixth sense of yours, don't you?"

I laughed, too. "I actually forgot all about that, but sure."

"How could you forget about the night you told me about your sixth sense? I mean, I keep reliving that mistletoe kiss in my head every time I look at you." He winked.

My cheeks flushed with heat. "You know, if you keep saying that, I might start to believe you."

"You say it as if I didn't enjoy it."

"Oh, I don't doubt you enjoyed it. But mostly because you were looking forward to torturing me with my mistake for the rest of my life."

He picked up his fork again and poked it into his salad. "So you think we're going to know each other for the rest of our lives, then?" He peeked up at me, and I didn't know if the twinkling Christmas lights in the restaurant were hitting him just right or what, but his eyes looked so blue that it made me lose my train of thought.

And when he kept staring at me, I realized he'd probably asked me a question that I could no longer remember.

I blinked my eyes. "What did you ask me again?"

He shook his head and looked down with a crooked smile on his lips. "Nothing important."

Then I remembered how he hadn't answered *my* question. "You still haven't told me what you think about your food," I said.

With a thoughtful expression, he chewed on the bite he'd just put in his mouth and followed it up with a sip of water. He said, "It's all right."

"Just all right?" I asked, my chest falling a little with disappointment.

"Okay, so it's kind of delicious and you might have just introduced me to my new favorite food."

"Really?" I raised my eyebrows. "It's even better than your precious Italian club sandwich?"

He grinned. "Even better than that. I think you just changed my life."

I laughed. "I don't know if I'd go that far." I poked my fork into my penne. "But I've always wanted to change someone's life."

We finished up our food a few minutes later and walked a few stores down to The Menswear Place.

"Ever been here before?" Logan asked as he held the door open for me.

"Nope," I said as I walked past him. "My dad has never tried to buy me a suit before."

Logan chuckled and followed me in. "Your dad always was a smart man."

"Yes, he is."

He stepped in front of me. "It's this way."

We came to a display table with ties of all sorts of colors laid out on it.

"So, you said your dress is pink and white?" He reached for a pink and white striped tie.

I shook my head and took it from his hand. "Did you not look at the photo I sent you? That is much too hot of a pink."

He held his hands up. "My mistake."

I rolled my eyes and smiled. "My dress is blush pink. It's a softer, more elegant pink."

"I never knew there was such a thing as blush pink," he mumbled.

"Well, looks like you just learned something new."

I studied the table and then smiled when I saw the perfect tie. It was pretty much the exact shade of pink as my dress. And the solid color would really pop against his tanned skin tone.

I lifted the tie and held it against Logan's chest to get an idea of how it would look on him. He seemed to go still as my hand touched the skin at the base of his neck.

I tried to keep my breathing even as I stood close to him. I didn't know why I kept being surprised at how attracted I was to Logan. It made perfect sense since I'd crushed on his brother for so long.

But I just kept surprising myself.

I cleared my throat, hoping he hadn't noticed how hard I was trying to keep my breathing even. "It goes well with your skin tone." I looked up at him. He had a nice neck. It was a masculine one but not too thick to be scary. I watched his Adam's apple bob.

Was he nervous?

I dared to meet his gaze, and when I did, he swallowed again. "D-do you think it will work?" he asked.

I looked away from his face and down to his chest, which probably was a mistake because his chest was also really nice. He could probably do a hundred pushups right here if I asked him to.

I shook those thoughts away. Why would I ask him to do something like that?

I made my mind come back to where it should be and realized I didn't need to hold the tie close to him anymore. So I pulled my hand away—forcing myself not to allow my fingers to graze along his chest as I did so.

"What color of suit were you planning to wear?" I folded the tie back up like the other ones on the table.

"I was thinking either my gray one or my blue one." He pushed his hands in his pockets. "Which do you think would be better?"

Oooh, I loved a good gray suit.

But I also loved a blue one, too. Plus, the blue would really bring out his eyes.

Not that I needed to have another reason to get caught staring into them. In fact, it would probably be better if he wore sunglasses that night. We'd be dancing, and I didn't need any romantic notions poking around in my head.

Unless he combed his hair like Jace does, and I could just pretend I was dancing with his brother.

Oooh, that could be nice.

But then I might accidentally call him Jace and that would probably ruin things. As much as I wanted to prove to Logan that him being nice for a whole night was an impossibility for him, I also didn't want to ruin the Christmas Ball. Last year, I'd had a stinky time at the ball. I didn't want it to be bad this year, too.

So I said, "You should just surprise me with whatever suit you choose. I'm sure either will be great with this tie."

He took the tie from my hands. "Great. I'll get this one then."

---

WHEN WE WALKED outside the store, it was softly snowing.

"How was it moving back to winter?" I asked Logan as I zipped up my coat. It had already been a super cold

December in Ridgewater, and I was so ready to go somewhere sunny and warm again.

Logan zipped his coat as well. "I actually don't mind the winter here. It mostly just snowed in the mountains in North Carolina, so I kind of missed it."

"Weirdo."

And I don't know what was wrong with him, but he cracked the cutest smile when I called him that.

Wow, that dimple in his left cheek was kind of adorable.

I made myself focus on the sidewalk with that thought, so I wouldn't be tempted to poke his dimple with my finger.

We walked a few businesses down until Logan stopped to look at a store window with the words "Emrie's Frozen Treats" on it.

"What's this place?" he asked.

"Oh, it's a cool ice cream shop that just opened last summer."

"Must be hard to keep customers coming in during the winter," Logan said as he peeked in through the window.

"I think it does okay. They have the best hot chocolate I've ever tasted."

He looked away from the window and back to me. "They do?"

"Yeah."

"Do you mind stopping in here? I have a weakness for hot chocolate."

I smiled. "You have a weakness for hot chocolate?"

He shrugged. "You say that like it's weird."

I laughed. "Let's see what you think of Emrie's."

We stepped inside the cute little shop that was like a throwback to the 50's with its fire-engine red booths and black-and-white checked tile flooring.

"Whoa," he said as he took in the place. "This is just like stepping back in time."

"I know. It's pretty cool."

Vintage Christmas music filled the air as we looked over the menu. They had gourmet hot chocolate in every flavor I could imagine. I'd gotten their cinnamon hot chocolate when I'd come here with Alyssa a couple of weeks ago after a basketball game. But when I saw the candy canes, I knew I had to get one of those in my hot chocolate today.

We were still waiting for the employee to come out of the back, when I heard a familiar laugh come from one of the booths.

And when I turned to see who it was, I froze. Sitting in a booth in the corner was Noah. And he was there with three other people. His best friend Easton, his girlfriend Lexi, and Juliette Cardini who I hadn't seen since last summer. She must have gotten back from Paris recently.

My gaze went back to Noah who had his arm around Lexi. I tried not to feel jealous that he had picked her over me. He said they'd been secretly dating for months, but I'd overheard someone in one of my classes this week whispering about how he'd heard Noah and Lexi had only started out faking a relationship because he didn't know how to tell me he wasn't interested.

My face burned just thinking about it.

Was I really so clueless that a person had to pretend to date someone else just to get me to move on?

And as if he'd been able to sense that I was thinking about him, Noah suddenly looked up from his conversation with his friends and caught me staring at him.

I scooted closer to Logan so we were side by side instead of me slightly behind him in line. And when I saw that Noah seemed to be watching us, like he was trying to figure out what Logan and I were to each other, I slipped my fingers into Logan's hand, which was just resting by his hip.

He turned to me, seeming surprised that I was holding his hand. And before he could say anything, I leaned close to his shoulder and whispered in his ear, "I promise I'll do anything you want if you just pretend that we're dating."

His lips spread into a wicked smile. "Anything?"

"Anything within reason." I shoved Logan in what I

hoped Noah would interpret as a flirtatious move if he noticed.

Logan winked. "Okay. How about you go ice skating with me tomorrow."

"What?" I pulled my head back.

"You said you'd do anything if I pretended to be your boyfriend. And so I'm saying I want you to go ice skating with me."

I shook my head. "I heard that part. I'm just confused about *why*."

He shrugged. "I like ice skating and don't want to go by myself."

I frowned, so confused. "So to get you to pretend like you're my boyfriend for a few minutes, you want to take me ice skating?"

He nodded. "That sounds about right."

Okay. Well, that wasn't what I was expecting at all. But I actually really liked ice skating, so it kind of seemed like a win-win.

Even if I did have to go with Logan.

He squeezed my hand, and I couldn't help but notice how nice it felt in mine. "So will you go ice skating with me, Raven?"

Was this some sort of trick?

I really had no idea what to make of this new version of Logan.

I shrugged and said, "That sounds like fun."

His smile stretched wide across his cheeks and he put his arm around my shoulder. "You're the best girlfriend, did you know that?"

My heart did a little flip-flop when he said the word *girlfriend*. No one had ever called me that before. But I worked hard to keep my reaction to myself. "Anything for you, *boyfriend*."

## CHAPTER EIGHT

WE GOT our hot chocolates to go and walked out of the shop, hand in hand. I expected Logan to let go once we were out of Noah's view, but he didn't. Instead, he simply adjusted his grip so it was more comfortable.

I didn't know if I should let him keep up the ruse, since we were most definitely not boyfriend and girlfriend, but then I told myself there was a possibility that Noah or his friends could see us as we walked down the street, so it would be best to hold hands all the way back to Logan's car.

"So what's up with that back there?" Logan asked after taking a sip of his drink. He had gone with the candy cane hot chocolate as well.

"Remember what Emily said in English on Monday?"

"About how you'd invited Noah Taylor to hang out after last week's game?"

I cringed at the memory. "I didn't just invite him to hang out. We made out at a party after he and Ashlyn Brooks broke up last summer. I thought it meant something, but apparently, it didn't." I shrugged. I was really good at doing that. I was terrible at reading guys true feelings, it seemed. "Anyway, since I'm the queen of rebound make-outs, I invited him to my house when he and Lexi broke up for like a second last Friday."

"And he said no?"

"Yup. Turned me down flat."

Logan winced. "Ouch."

"Yep."

A cool gust of air whipped down the sidewalk, blowing snow in my eyes. I ducked my head down to blink the snow away.

Once the wind had slowed and I could breathe again, I said, "You want to know the most embarrassing part?"

A crooked grin lifted Logan's lips. "I always like hearing embarrassing stories about you."

I rolled my eyes. "I thought you would." I took a sip from my hot chocolate. It was the perfect temperature: not too hot, not too cold. "The most embarrassing part of this whole thing is that I heard they started dating just to get me to move on."

I ran my finger around the lid on my cup, feeling the shame pour over me once again.

Instead of laughing, Logan just stared at me with surprise in his expression. "What?"

I tilted my head to the side and lifted a shoulder. "At first I kind of suspected it, since Noah never went for girls like her before. But I guess Lexi must have had something in her that Noah couldn't find in me."

Something no guy seemed to find in me.

I didn't get it. I wasn't ugly. I wasn't stupid either, so I figured I was interesting enough to talk to. And I'd kissed enough guys to know that they liked it.

So what else was missing? What else did I need to finally get a guy to want me for more than just a night of kissing?

Logan peered down at me as we walked down the sidewalk, and I worried he was going to have an answer to my questions. If anyone could tell me what my flaws were, I was sure it was Logan.

He cleared his throat and gave my hand a gentle squeeze. "Don't take it personally, Raven. Just because Noah Taylor picked someone over you, doesn't mean every guy would."

"Thanks for saying that." I tried to say it lightly, but my voice cracked.

He stopped walking and stood so we were facing each

other. "As someone who messed up a lot of things in my life because I was constantly comparing myself to another person, I can tell you that it's not you. People just vibe better with certain personalities."

I nodded. I guessed that made sense.

I wanted to ask him about why he always compared himself to someone else—that someone else who I assumed was his twin brother—when he started walking again and looked over at me with a lighthearted expression.

"So, not to turn the tables and rub it in your face about how you're not the only one getting rebound kisses, but I do need to point out that it kind of sounds like *I* was your rebound kiss on Friday."

I hadn't thought about it like that, but now that Logan mentioned it... "I guess you kind of were. Sorry you had to find out that not only did I think you were Jace, but I was also on the rebound."

He glanced down at our hands. "Are you only holding my hand still because you're imagining I'm actually Jace?" He raised his eyebrows.

My jaw dropped. How had he known I'd just been thinking about something like that when we'd been in the tie store?

He narrowed his gaze. "Raven?"

I scrunched up my face. He totally caught me. "Okay,

so maybe for a second I considered pretending you were Jace."

It was his turn to look shocked and offended.

I hurried to say, "But I decided that would be stupid. So really, you've been Logan in my head this whole time."

He let go of my hand, and I worried I'd really hurt his feelings. He reached in his pocket and pulled out his keys to unlock his Corvette.

The low rumble of the engine started when we were about ten feet away.

"Hey, don't be mad at me. You said yourself last week that you're on the rebound and that I better not get confused and start liking you. So why should you care if I imagined your brother, anyway?"

He looked at me sideways. "So you're just trying to follow my rule?"

I'd go with that. "Yep."

And it was a good thing I'd just remembered his rule because my brain was already tempted to think he was cute and nice and funny and...

I shook my head. Yep, I didn't need to start getting confused into thinking Logan was actually likable in that kind of way.

"So what is it that you like so much about my brother, anyway? I know you've said he's way nicer, but I've been pretty nice to you all week. What else does he have that I don't?"

Why did he want to know?

Was it because he and Jace always had some sort of competition going? Or because he really wanted to know why I liked Jace but not him?

We made it to his car and he opened the door for me to climb in. I set my cup in one of the cup holders and tried to think of how to answer Logan's question as I buckled in.

He climbed inside a moment later and turned up the heater, letting his hands rest above the vents.

"Are you avoiding my question?" he asked after a moment.

I shrugged. "No, I'm just trying to think of an answer."

He nodded and looked ahead at the cars parked in front of us. "And is anything coming to mind?"

I sighed. Now that I'd spent a little time with Logan, he really didn't get on my nerves as badly as he used to. And I'd spent zero time with Jace since he'd been back, so I had no idea if I really even liked him anymore, or just the memory of liking him.

Logan turned to me again, waiting for an answer. Finally, I shrugged and said, "I guess you aren't as bad as I remember."

He narrowed his eyes as if to study me, and I couldn't help but feel nervous under his stare.

What did Logan Carmichael see when he looked at me?

After another long moment, he said, "Well, that's good to know. You're not as bad as I remember, either."

And I knew it wasn't exactly a compliment, but I was suddenly having a hard time breathing.

---

BEFORE WE COULD PULL out of the parking spot, Logan's phone dinged. He pulled it out of his back pocket, and when he looked at the screen his expression fell.

"What is it?" I asked, suddenly concerned.

"Jace just bailed on me."

"He did?"

He nodded. "We were supposed to go look for a Christmas tree at five, but apparently he's still goofing around with Trey and Chance in Syracuse."

"I'm sure you guys could get one later."

"We could, but I was hoping to get one before all the good ones were taken." He put his phone back in his pocket. "Maybe I'll just go by myself. Jace wasn't super interested in going, anyway."

"I could go with you if you wanted company." The words were out of my mouth before I realized it.

Was I seriously offering to spend even more time with him today?

"Really?" he said before I could take back my offer. "The tree lot's not too far from here. I looked it up this morning."

"Sure, no problem," I said, not believing I was even doing this. "I'll just text my mom and tell her I'll be home later."

Logan turned on some music as we drove to the tree lot. I'd expected some sort of rap music, like what he used to boom through his bedroom windows back when we were neighbors. But this music was actually pretty good.

"Who is this?" I pointed to the stereo.

"It's this indie band I just discovered called *Walk Off the Earth*. I love their remake of *Girls Like You*." He pushed a button on the stereo a couple of times and turned the volume up. Soon the sound of someone picking a ukulele filled the speaker.

A slow smile slipped up my lips as I listened. "I love this song." I leaned back in the seat to get comfortable as a male voice started singing.

Logan looked over at me and grinned but didn't say anything, and we just listened to the music as we drove through the slush-covered streets.

And I couldn't help but smile over the fact that I was even in this position.

If anyone had asked me a week ago if I'd ever drive around with Logan Carmichael while listening to awesome music, I would have said no way. But apparently, my life wanted to laugh at me because right now, there was no place I'd rather be.

But as much as I was enjoying this, I knew I needed to remember that we were just friends. I didn't need this to turn out like every other time I thought I had a connection with a guy: real to me but just a fun time for them.

---

"DOES your family usually buy a real tree?" I asked Logan as we walked through the gate to the tree lot.

"My mom usually insists on artificial trees, since she likes them to be perfectly symmetrical and professionally decorated. But Jace and I were able to convince her to let us get a real tree for our suite."

Their suite? Exactly what kind of a house did they live in?

"Do you guys live in a hotel?"

He furrowed his brow. "No?"

"You said you and Jace have a suite. I've only heard of hotels and office buildings having suites."

"Oh, no. Nothing like that." Logan nodded to the guy working the lot when we walked past. "We have our own sitting room next to our bedrooms. Kind of like a mini apartment, I guess."

That must be some house. Pretty sure we just had plain old bedrooms and shared bathrooms at my home.

"You'll have to show me this suite of yours sometime," I said.

"You want to see my bedroom?" He cocked his eyebrow. "Apparently, I've been a much nicer boy than I thought." He winked.

The blood drained from my cheeks and I stumbled when I realized how bad that sounded. "I didn't mean that." My eyes widened. "I may make out with random guys at parties, but I'm not that kind of a girl."

He grinned. "I was joking, Raven. I knew what you meant."

I shook my head and continued forward. "I guess I deserved that after teasing you about your elf costume all last week."

He grinned. "Um, yeah."

We walked down a narrow trail and the scent of fir trees filled my senses. My family never got live trees, since the one year we had gotten one, we ended up with a bunch of bugs crawling around our living room. Since then, I'd begged my parents to never do that again because

I was scared of bugs crawling in my bed at night. But I loved their woodsy scent. It reminded me of camping with my grandparents when I was little.

"What size were you thinking of getting?" I asked

Logan stopped and pursed his lips as he looked over the options in front of us. "Maybe a seven-foot tree?" He raised an arm above his head. "About this high."

After deciding that none of the trees in front of us were right, we continued down the path. Logan would pause every now and then to inspect a tree more closely. And every time he was considering one, he would put his hands on his hips and get this really serious but cute look on his face.

"What about this one?" I asked when I found one about the height he'd indicated. It was a beautiful, dark green tree with full branches.

Logan came to stand by me. His breath was visible in the cold December air, his nose turning pink from the chill.

"I like it. We may come back to it later."

He took a picture of the tag with the tree number and then we continued down the row.

When we came to a fork in the path, Logan turned one way and I went down the other. A minute later I found another tree that looked really nice. It wasn't the perfectly symmetrical type that his mother preferred;

instead, this had a little twist in the middle of its trunk. It had character, and when I thought about it some more, it seemed like the kind of tree Logan would be if he was one. A little rough around the edges, but once you actually tried to get to know him, he was surprisingly pleasant to be around.

"What do you think about this one?" I called in his general direction as I pulled on the branches to get a better look. But I must have loosened up the tree beside it, because before I knew what was happening, a huge tree fell on me, knocking me down.

I landed hard on the frozen ground, my hands barely catching my fall before my face could collide with the wet gravel. *Ouch.*

I tried to push myself up onto my knees so I could get out from beneath the tree, but it was too heavy.

Running footsteps headed toward me, and a moment later, Logan's face was close to mine. "Are you okay?" he asked, anxiety in his voice.

I squeezed my eyes shut, urging the pain in my banged-up hands and knees to leave. "I'm okay."

"How did that happen?" Logan immediately grabbed the huge tree and lifted it off of me.

Once I was free, I drew in a deep breath, feeling like I could actually breathe again. "I moved the other tree and I guess that must've knocked this one loose or something."

After Logan set the tree back in its spot, he held his hand out for me. "Here, let me help you up," he said.

I took his hand and let him lift me to my feet.

He gasped. "You're bleeding."

I looked at my hand, which he was still holding. Sure enough, I had scratches all over it. It wasn't horrible, but I would need to clean it up.

As if reading my thoughts, Logan said, "My house is just a couple of minutes away. Let's go and get you cleaned up. I can get a tree later. I would have had to pick it up in my truck later, anyway."

I nodded, feeling stupid that I even fell in the first place. But Logan wasn't laughing at me and my clumsiness, so at least that was good.

## CHAPTER NINE

FIVE MINUTES LATER, we drove up to what I liked to call the "rich district" of Ridgewater. The neighborhood where Kelsie Perkins and Chance Clemont lived. The houses were huge up here, the lots spacious.

I had expected the Carmichaels to be well off after seeing Logan's Corvette, but when we drove up to a sprawling white mansion, my jaw literally dropped.

"This is where you live now?" I asked when he stopped at a big wrought-iron gate and punched in a security code.

"Yep. Home, sweet home," he said in a sarcastic tone.

The gates slowly opened, and Logan drove down the long asphalt drive lined with tall snow-covered trees. The home's white exterior glistened in the late-afternoon sunlight, as if the paint had diamonds in it.

Logan had a look of apprehension in his eyes as he studied my reaction. "What do you think?"

I just sat there and stared at the expansiveness of it all. "It's beautiful. And I'm pretty sure my house could fit in yours about three times."

He shook his head. "My mom went a little overboard."

He rolled his car the rest of the way toward the house and into one of the many garages.

"How's your hand?" he asked once he'd parked and turned off his car.

My hand was wrapped in a napkin that he'd had in his glove compartment. "It hurts. But it's not bleeding as bad as it was."

"Let's go clean it up."

I followed him through the garage and past several other fancy vehicles. There was a Ferrari, an Escalade, and what I guessed must be Jace's Tesla. "Have you guys added more people to your family since you've been gone?" I asked.

He furrowed his brow. "No."

I counted at least six vehicles, most of them on the high-end. But there was one that didn't fit: an older Toyota Corolla that was at the last garage door opening. "Whose car is that?"

Logan looked back to where I pointed and shrugged. "That's Pam's."

"And who's Pam?" He'd said they hadn't added anyone to their family.

"She's our housekeeper-slash-cook."

This was so out of my league.

I followed him through the door in front of the Escalade and we walked into what I guessed was a super fancy version of a mudroom. Logan sat down on a bench and started taking off his shoes, so I did the same.

Once our shoes were off, Logan led me into the huge kitchen that had tall white cupboards, white granite countertops, and a huge curved bar.

"We usually keep the first-aid kit in the main bathroom," he said.

I took in the high ceilings, the plush carpet, and expensive-looking furniture as we passed through the different rooms of the house.

"Did you guys really just move here last week?" I asked, confused.

Logan looked back to me as he walked down the hall. "Yeah, why?"

I shrugged. "I was just expecting to see a lot more boxes everywhere. It looks like you guys have lived here forever."

Logan switched on the light in the bathroom. "My mom had the movers set everything up before we moved in. She can't stand to have boxes to unpack or things out of their regular place."

Logan dug through a few drawers and cupboards before eventually coming out with the prettiest first-aid kit I'd ever seen. It wasn't the typical tackle box like my family had, with the words "first-aid" written in permanent marker across the top. Instead, it was a chic, teal rectangular metal box with fancy latches on the front.

"How about you wash your hand first and then we can get you all fixed up." Logan looked up at me briefly as he dug through the contents of the kit.

I switched on the expensive-looking nickel-coated faucet and washed my hands. The water turned pink as the blood washed off.

I shook my hands to try and dry them, not wanting the new blood that was resurfacing from my cuts to stain the nice plush towel hanging on the hook on the wall.

Logan must have noticed what I was doing and said, "Go ahead and use the towel. We have plenty."

I took the white towel off of the hook and patted my hands with it. Even the towel felt expensive. It was thick and soft. I kind of wanted to lift it to my nose and see if their fabric softener smelled expensive, too—but decided that would be weird. I wrapped the towel around the cuts and waited.

Once Logan had located all the things he needed to

fix me up, he stepped closer. The light scent of winter air clinging to his skin met my nose.

"Let's see what we can do." Logan carefully removed the towel from my hand, his fingers lightly brushing across my skin.

"Looks like the tree scraped you up pretty good," Logan said as he gently ran his thumb across the back of my hand.

I held my breath as goosebumps raced across my skin from his light touch. And when he looked at me, my breath caught in my throat. I really hoped he hadn't noticed the way his touch affected me.

He swallowed, his Adam's apple shifting. "Let's sanitize this first." And when he slowly let go of my hand, it almost seemed like he didn't want to.

But of course that could have just been my imagination. I imagined things like this all the time with guys.

He made quick work of putting alcohol on a cotton ball and then turned back, regarding me with cautious eyes.

"This might sting a little." He took my hand again and gently ran the cotton ball along the scratches. I gasped at the cool feeling, and he asked, "Is that okay?"

My words suddenly fled me, so I nodded. We were so close, and he smelled so amazingly good. And I couldn't help but think about how gently he was treating me. I'd never had a guy take care of me before.

When I could finally speak again, I managed to say, "It was just cold. I'm fine."

So much for not being affected by him.

He finished with the cotton ball a moment later and then pulled out the triple antibiotic ointment. He squeezed the glob along the cut. "Go ahead and rub that in," he said.

I did as he said, my fingers shaking with nerves.

"How's your other hand?" he asked.

I lifted it, urging it to hold still so he wouldn't realize how nervous he made me, and while there were no scrapes or cuts, my wrist did look swollen.

"I think I landed on it funny," I said.

He nodded. "I think so too." Then he dug through the first-aid kit again and came out with an ace bandage. "Let's go into the kitchen so you can sit down while I wrap that for you."

I nodded and released a shaky breath. "Okay."

What was happening to me? I was acting like I'd never been this close to a guy before.

In the kitchen, he pulled a chair out from the rectangular table. "You sit. I'll grab an ice pack, and then we can take care of that."

He went over to the fridge, opening the freezer side

door. After rummaging around for a bit, he came out with an ice pack.

"Hopefully this will help," he said. Then he pulled out a chair for himself and scooted it closer so we sat knee to knee.

And I didn't know why, since it was only our knees touching, but my legs were suddenly super wobbly and shaky.

I needed to stop thinking about my reactions to him because it was making me have even more reactions. And I couldn't be attracted to Logan. He was just being nice to me to prove he could be nice. He didn't actually *like* me.

I sighed. But it was hard not to be attracted to him when he'd been nothing but fun, and flirty, and wonderful since he'd come back.

Sure he'd tricked me on Friday night, but he'd also kissed me. And that kiss had been amazing...even if it had been under false pretenses.

I watched him as he wrapped my wrist. Was it wrong of me to want to try kissing him again? To see how it went if I thought he was himself instead of his brother?

I shook my head. I needed to stop thinking about that, especially when I was sitting knee to knee with him and he was bent over so our faces were less than a foot apart.

So I brought my mind back to the present moment.

His long, agile fingers worked quickly as they circled my hand and wrist with the beige bandage.

"You're really good at this," I said, hoping small talk would help me remember that he was still on the rebound and I didn't get involved with rebound guys, anymore.

He peeked at me and gave me a half smile. "I've had to do this a few times."

"Yeah?"

He concentrated on what he was doing. "Remember when Jace and I were really into skateboarding in middle school?"

I nodded, picturing how they used to ride down our quiet street most afternoons after school and their mom would always yell at them to get out of the road because it was dangerous.

He lifted a shoulder. "We fell enough times that I got really good at this."

"Are you guys still as close as you were back then?"

He shrugged. "I don't know. We're probably a little too competitive now."

"Really?" I asked, intrigued. "What kinds of things do you compete for these days?" I knew they'd been into basketball before they moved, but was there something else?

He finished bandaging my wrist and set the icepack on top of it. "Mostly just girls."

"So did Jace go after your ex in Sweet Water, too?" I asked. And I don't know why, but a strange, intense feeling of jealousy at the reminder that he was still getting over her pushed its way into my chest.

"Yeah. We both went after Olivia, but for once I actually won. Though in hindsight, it would've probably been better if she'd picked Jace."

"Let me guess: she was a tall, leggy blonde with blue eyes."

Logan had always gone after that type in the past.

He shook his head and laughed. "You know me so well."

*Dang it.*

But then he leaned closer and spoke in a low, seductive voice, "But these days, I go for the dark-haired girls with chocolate brown eyes."

My throat threatened to close up when his gaze dipped down to my lips.

Was he hinting at something?

Should I be reading into this?

His gaze lifted to my eyes again, and my heart took off like a race horse. He was so unbelievably good-looking.

The sound of the garage door opening broke the lock our eyes had, and when I turned to see who had found me getting lost in Logan's eyes, I saw his brother.

## CHAPTER TEN

"HI, JACE," I said awkwardly as I quickly stood from my chair, my face turning red.

Jace looked from me to his twin with a curious expression. Had he noticed how close Logan and I had been a second before?

"Hey, Raven." Jace hung his coat on a hook in their mudroom and walked into the kitchen. "What are you doing here?"

He narrowed his eyes at Logan as if trying to figure out why his brother and I were alone in their house. As far as he knew, we still hated each other.

I picked up the ice pack that had dropped to the ground when I'd stood. "We were looking for a Christmas tree, but I ended up getting attacked by one. Logan brought me here to fix me up." I awkwardly held the ice pack to my wrist as I lifted it for him to see.

Jace glanced at my bandaged wrist and shrugged. "Cool. I mean, sorry you got hurt."

"It's okay."

Then I turned to Logan who had a frustrated look on his face for a moment before he smoothed it away. And I just felt super awkward as the boys stood there watching each other and watching me. Was Logan embarrassed that he was found alone in his house with me?

Logan cleared his throat after a while and said to Jace, "I guess now that you're back we can go get that tree."

"Okay. Sure." Jace grabbed his coat from a hook and shrugged back into it.

Logan turned to me. "We can drop you off at your house first, if you like."

I pushed a smile on my face. "That would be great. My mom's probably wondering where I've been all day."

Logan and I put on our coats and shoes in silence, neither of us saying anything about the moment we'd had. Had he been thinking about kissing me? He'd looked at my lips, right?

I shook my head. I didn't need to wonder about that. I'd probably just imagined it.

Logan grabbed a set of keys off of a hook on the wall.

"I think we'll take the truck. It'll be easier to attach the tree on top of that, anyway."

I walked toward their Toyota Tundra but stopped when I realized it wasn't one of those huge four-door trucks. Instead, it just had a regular cab with a single row of seats. Which meant I would most likely be squished in the middle of the Carmichael twins.

My old self would be jumping up and down at the prospect of sitting so close to Jace, but with the awkwardness between us all, I was expecting a long drive back to my house.

Logan stopped behind me, his chest brushing against my back. "Is the truck okay?" he asked in a quiet voice that made chills race up the back of my neck.

"The truck's fine." I craned my neck to look at him, letting my gaze travel over his face. Wow, he was hot.

Logan opened the driver's side door and gestured for me to climb in. I scooted into the middle and both boys sat on either side.

It was a tight fit, and when I went to buckle myself in beside Logan, I misjudged the angle of the latch and totally swiped his butt with my fingers instead.

"Sorry," I said, feeling my face turn deep red.

He cast me a flirtatious look. "Don't be." And when he winked, I could have died.

I pinched my lips together and tried again. This time I got it right and there was no unnecessary butt-touching.

Logan backed out of the garage and soon we were all driving down the road.

"Do you and Alyssa still hang out as much as you used to?" Jace asked me after a minute, breaking the silence that had fallen over the cab.

"We're still best friends, so yeah."

"You guys have any fun plans for tonight?"

I frowned. Why was he asking this? "No. She's going on a date with Trey."

"She is?" He frowned.

"Yeah..." I said the word slowly. "They go out every Saturday night." Was he surprised because he didn't think they went on dates, or for some other reason?

He shrugged. "Good for them."

I went back to watching the road.

At a stop light, Logan shifted in his seat, causing his thigh to press against mine. Warmth immediately radiated up my leg, and I couldn't help but wonder if it was his way of pointing out to me that he was still in the truck.

Was he jealous that I was talking to Jace? Was it wrong of me to hope that he was?

Jace spoke again, "Did Logan give you a tour of our house?"

"No. We just got there a little before you did."

"He at least showed you the pool, right?" Jace asked.

I turned to Logan. "You guys have a pool?"

The light turned green, so Logan pulled forward. "Yeah."

"Like an indoor pool? Because if it's outside, we could totally just go ice skating back there tomorrow."

He looked at me from the corner of his eye, a slight smile on his lip. "It's indoor."

"You guys are going ice skating?" Jace's expression brightened. "I haven't been ice skating in forever."

"Yeah, *Raven and I* are going skating." I didn't miss how Logan emphasized the part about it just being me and him, and it made my heart flutter that he was slightly possessive of me.

But apparently Jace missed it, because he said, "You know what we should do? We should go ice skating, get all cold, and then go back to our house afterwards for a pool and hot tub party."

I peeked at Logan to see what he thought. A pool and hot tub party did sound fun.

But I didn't want to ruin any plans Logan had for tomorrow. He didn't seem like he wanted Jace to be there for some reason.

"What do you think, Logan?" I asked. "I'm okay with it just being us."

He sighed. "Jace can come."

"What about Alyssa?" Jace asked. And when I furrowed my brow, he added, "I mean, I just figured since you two are best friends you'd probably want to invite her."

"Alyssa can come, too," Logan said.

We turned onto my street, and a moment later, Logan pulled up to the curb in front of my house. He climbed out of his door and let me slide out behind him.

I looked at Logan, feeling awkward that Jace was just a few feet away. "I had fun today."

He glanced over to Jace, and I couldn't help but feel that he also didn't like the fact that his brother was watching us. "It was fun. Thanks for helping me find a tie."

I fiddled with the zipper at the bottom of my coat. "Well, I guess I'll see you tomorrow."

"Yeah." He rubbed the back of his neck. "Do you want me to pick you up before heading to the ice rink, or do you think you'll come with Alyssa?"

"Oh," I said, trying to decide. I really wanted to ride with Logan because we'd had such a great time together today and his car was awesome. But I didn't want him to think I expected him to give me special treatment after today. "I should probably ride with Alyssa, I guess."

He nodded, but I imagined I saw disappointment in his eyes. He gripped the truck door, and I had the sudden urge to give him a hug. It was strange, since I'd never wanted to hug Logan before, but it just seemed like after today, we had grown closer. Close enough to start doing these things.

But he climbed in before I could get up the courage to make it happen. "Should we meet at the skating rink around one?" he asked.

I nodded. "Yeah. And if Alyssa can't come, I'll call you for a ride."

That earned me a smile. "See you tomorrow."

I walked to the sidewalk and waited until they drove off before walking inside. And as I watched the taillights disappear down the road, I realized something.

I might be starting to like Logan.

## CHAPTER ELEVEN

ALYSSA and I arrived at the skating rink at exactly one o'clock the next day. I wore blue jeans with gray leg warmers and the red coat I usually wore when I went running. I'd put my hair in a high ponytail to keep it out of my face, and I might have taken extra care on my make-up this morning.

The swelling in my wrist had gone down and it felt a lot better. I rolled the bandage up and put it in my backpack with my swimming stuff so I could give it back to Logan.

*Logan.*

I smiled just thinking his name.

"What are you smiling about?" Alyssa asked me as we walked up the sidewalk to the skating rink's entrance.

"No reason," I said too quickly.

She lifted an eyebrow. "I don't buy it. What exactly did you do yesterday?"

I didn't know if I wanted to talk about hanging out with Logan all day, since I still didn't understand it all myself. But I said, "Me and Logan kind of hung out all afternoon."

Her jaw dropped. "You and Logan? Like, Logan Carmichael?"

I nodded. "Yeah."

"And?" She waited for me to say more.

I shrugged. "And it was nice. He was nice."

We reached the entrance then, and just before she pulled the door open, she asked, "Do you like him?"

I bit my lip and tried to keep the butterflies at bay as I thought about my answer. But the butterflies wanted to wake up. "I might."

She raised her eyebrows. "Wow."

"I know." Then I hurried to say, "But I need your help. As you know, I've been super bad at reading guys, so I was hoping you could maybe watch Logan today and help me figure out if he likes me? I don't want to have another Noah Taylor situation."

She looked through the glass doors, and I noticed that the boys were right at the front of the lobby. Excitement bubbled inside my chest with the anticipation of spending another afternoon with Logan.

"Sure. I'll watch him." She turned back to me.

I grinned. "Thanks."

She pulled on the door and we stepped into the skating rink lobby. The guys stood from the benches, and I met Logan with a tentative smile, butterflies flapping around in my stomach. I had expected him to return my smile, but instead, he just greeted me with a stony expression.

Had he somehow heard my conversation with Alyssa?

My heart, which had swelled over the past minute, shriveled up with the thought that he had and that he didn't like the possibility of me liking him.

Before he could notice how his scowl affected me, I turned my gaze to Jace, who was smiling hugely at Alyssa and me.

Well, at least someone was happy to see us.

Jace clapped his hands together. "We already took care of your admission and skates, so we can just head downstairs."

"You guys didn't have to do that," I hurried to say, looking anxiously at Logan. Was he acting weird because he hadn't wanted this to look like a date?

Jace shook his head and handed us our wristbands and vouchers for the skates. "It's no problem at all. We invited you, so it all works out."

Well, technically, Logan had invited me because I'd

asked him to pretend to be my boyfriend for a minute, and Jace had invited himself and Alyssa, but I wouldn't argue with him. I didn't need a second twin scowling at me.

Alyssa and I put our purple wristbands on, and then we all walked down the stairs to get our skates. Logan and I somehow ended up side by side, but he didn't say anything, which just made me feel so awkward that I couldn't think of anything to say to make things normal between us again.

Had I totally imagined everything yesterday?

"Have you guys been skating yet this winter?" Jace asked after we got our skates and went to the benches outside the rink to put them on.

"Not yet," Alyssa answered.

I tied my laces around my white skates. "I haven't been, either."

Jace glanced at Logan who was shoving his left foot into one of his black skates. "Me and Mr. Grumpy over here haven't been since before we moved away, so it should be pretty fun."

Logan glared at Jace at his mention of him being "Mr. Grumpy." I made quick work of tying up my other skate, so I could get on the ice and away from Logan and whatever was bothering him.

After putting on my thin gloves, I glided onto the ice. I

waited for Alyssa and Jace to join me, and then we started skating around the rink.

"What's up with Logan?" I asked Jace, once we had circled about a quarter of the way. Logan was still sitting on the bench, taking his time lacing up his skates.

Jace glanced back at his brother. "He's upset about something my mom told him this morning."

"So it has nothing to do with me?"

Jace got a confused look on his face and asked, "Why would it have anything to do with you?"

"No reason."

We finished our first circle around the rink when Logan stood up from his seat. "You guys go ahead, I'm going to wait for Logan." Jace and Alyssa looked awkwardly at each other for a second but continued forward.

I slowed down to wait for him on the side.

"You decided to join us after all?" I asked when he got to me.

"Yeah, sorry I'm weird today."

I pushed off the wall and skated slowly beside him. "Why is that?"

I hoped he felt he could confide in me. I'd like to think that we were becoming friends.

He wobbled as he skated forward. "Apparently, my

mom invited Olivia and her family to a housewarming dinner at our house on Friday."

"Olivia, as in your ex?" My insides turned cold.

He sighed heavily. "Yeah."

"And that's bad?" I asked, hopefully.

He shrugged. "It's just weird. I was finally getting over her."

"Oh, so you broke up pretty recently then?"

He nodded. "Yeah, just a few weeks before we moved here."

Wow, that was recent. How did I not know about this? I knew he said I couldn't fall in love with him because he'd just gotten out of a relationship. But I hadn't realized that he was on the rebound.

Had I really let myself fall for another guy who was trying to get over someone else? If that wasn't the story of my life, I didn't know what was.

"So are you worried all your old feelings will come back when you see her?" I asked, though I hated that I even had to ask that question.

He shook his head. "No. I just don't want to see her."

"Yeah?"

We skated a few strides in silence before he said, "It was never going to work."

I didn't know if that was better or worse. Was it better that he might hate her now? Or worse that he might forgive her because he could still have feelings for her?

Man, this would have been good to know a week ago.

"Sorry to hear that."

He shrugged. "Don't be. It just got me in a weird mood. But I think it actually helped to talk to you about it."

"Well, that's good." Good for him anyway. But now I was totally going to be second guessing everything he said or did.

I pushed off my left foot to go faster, deciding to just let it drop. If he said he felt better, I'd go with it.

I expected him to pick up his speed as I went faster, but when I turned back, he was still going super slow.

"Did you forget how to skate?" I asked, changing the subject. Maybe if I started acting like we used to always act together, I would feel better.

He grinned, his dimple appearing on his left cheek. "Actually, I never was very good at it."

"But I thought you Carmichael boys were good at everything," I taunted.

It did feel better to talk smack to him.

He chuckled. "We play basketball in the winter. Not hockey."

"Well, you better get really good really fast because I think it's time for us to have a race."

"Right now?" he asked.

I nodded. "Yep. Right now."

He chuckled. "I never knew you were so competitive."

I shrugged, and to show off a little, I did a 180-degree turn and started skating backwards. "You don't compete in gymnastics for six years without being a little competitive."

"So do you really want to race me right now?"

"Yep." I did. I could use the distraction from my worries.

We went to the top of the rink and waited for a few of the families to pass us. "First one to the other side wins, okay?" I said.

"Okay." There was a competitive glint in his eye.

"On your mark," I said. "Get set."

"Go."

He shot forward before I had a chance to realize that he'd just said go. So I pushed forward on my skates as fast as I could. I caught up to him quickly, and I was about to pass him when he suddenly grabbed me around the waist and said, "Oh no, you don't."

I didn't know what he'd expected to accomplish by pulling me back to him, but in a split second we were crashing to the ground in a heap of legs and arms and skates.

"Ow," I said, pushing myself off his chest and rubbing my head where it had hit his solid shoulder in our fall.

Logan just lay there on his back with his head on the ice, breathing heavily. "Sorry," he panted. "I just couldn't lose to a girl."

My jaw dropped. "I can't believe you just said that." I smacked his bicep playfully. "You jerk."

His chest started shaking as he laughed, quietly at first and then loudly. "I'm joking, Raven."

I rolled my eyes and sat up straighter. My legs and butt were starting to go numb on the ice. "So did you accomplish what you wanted with that slick move of yours?"

He propped himself up on his elbows and gave me a suggestive look. "I just wanted to be close to you."

I smacked him again.

Logan sat up and got a funny expression on his face. Then he tilted to the side and reached a hand to his butt. "I think I split my pants."

I craned my neck to try and get a peek at his backside. Sure enough, there was a split about three inches long down the back of his jeans—and showing through the tear was red and green striped underwear.

"Are you wearing Christmas underwear?" I asked, trying to get a better look.

His eyes went wide, and he sat back down so both of

his butt cheeks were on the ice. "You weren't supposed to see that."

I laughed. "I never pegged you for the kind of guy that would wear festive underwear."

He shook his head. "They're my lucky underwear. I don't typically wear boxer briefs with Christmas colors, if you must know."

"Sure."

He rolled his eyes and got on his hands and knees before standing up.

It was then that I noticed a bunch of people looking at us, and I had to smile. "I think I'm having déjà vu," I said.

He held his hand out to me. I took it and let him pull me up. "And what's giving you déjà vu? The fact that I helped you up yesterday, too, because you can't seem to stay upright on a cold surface?"

"Hey." I scowled.

"What? You don't like it when people make fun of you after an accidental fall?"

I stepped forward until we were inches apart. "I was thinking more like how the last time we were in front of a bunch of families with young children, you gave everyone an eyeful then, too."

He looked around to see what I was talking about, and his face paled when he saw a bunch of little kids pointing and giggling at seeing his underwear.

"I think it's time for me to go home and hang out in the hot tub. I have a feeling I'm going to be a little bruised from that fall."

"If not your body, then your ego, right?"

"Har-har." He held his hand out to me. "Let's get out of here."

## CHAPTER TWELVE

ALYSSA AND JACE didn't feel like leaving the rink just yet, so we told them we'd see them later at the house so Logan could stop flashing everyone with his underwear. I grabbed my bag out of Alyssa's car and we went ahead and drove to Logan's house in his Corvette.

When we walked inside, Mrs. Carmichael was in the kitchen, hovering over a cookbook with the woman who I assumed was their housekeeper, Pam.

"Hey, Mom," Logan said as he took off his shoes.

Mrs. Carmichael was a tall, willowy woman with stunning blonde hair and blue eyes. She looked up from the cookbook. "Hi, Logan. Back already?"

"Yeah." He turned around to show her his backside. "I had a little accident."

"Oh my word, Logan." Mrs. Carmichael put a hand to

her chest and looked up to the ceiling, like the last thing she wanted to see was her seventeen-year-old son's choice of underwear. "Please go put some pants on."

Logan chuckled, apparently enjoying upsetting his mother. "We're actually going to go swimming, so I'll put on my swim trunks instead."

Mrs. Carmichael's gaze landed on me, and it only took a moment for recognition to show on her face. "Raven Rodgers?" she asked, coming closer.

I dipped my head forward in a nod. "Yeah. It's good to see you again."

She gave me a hug, and then she pulled away and held me at arm's length. "My, you've grown since the last time I saw you. You've turned into a very beautiful young lady. Don't you think so, Logan?" She turned to her son, and I could have died of embarrassment.

But when I looked to see how horrified he must be, I found a quiet look instead. Did I dare to hope that there was admiration in his eyes?

He cleared his throat. "Yes, she's very beautiful."

*Very beautiful.*

I let the words linger in my mind for a moment.

Mrs. Carmichael clasped her hands together. "Well, I better get back to planning Friday night's menu with Pam. You two have fun."

And with the reminder about their Friday night

dinner with Logan's ex-girlfriend, the high I'd momentarily been on after he'd said I was beautiful instantly died.

When his mom went back to the cookbook, Logan turned to me. "Before we go to the pool, do you want to see the tree we picked out?"

I shrugged. "Sure."

Logan led me down a hall and then up a beautiful staircase with white carpeted stairs and wrought-iron railings. I studied his broad shoulders as I followed him. Logan had really nice shoulders. I wondered what it would feel like to run my hands across them.

Then an image of his ex-girlfriend running her fingers over his shoulders popped into my head and I was no longer curious what it would feel like.

"This is it," Logan said when we made it to a room just off the top of the stairs. The afternoon sunlight shone through the sheer curtains as he led me further inside. There was a TV, a couch, and a loveseat, and in the corner was their tree.

"Do you recognize it?" Logan asked.

I took a closer look and smiled. "It's the crooked one."

He stepped to my side and pressed his hand against my lower back, bending close to my ear and whispering, "I figured I should probably get it after all the trouble it caused you."

I looked at the crooked trunk. "It actually reminded me of you," I said. "That's why I wanted to show it to you in the first place."

"It reminded you of *me?*" he asked, seeming surprised and slightly confused.

I nodded. "Yeah."

"And why do you think I look like a crooked tree?"

I laughed. "I don't think you look like a tree. I just..." I sighed, trying to figure out how to word it without giving away too much. I couldn't let him know that I was starting to like him. "I guess it reminded me of you because you're a little rough around the edges, but once you let people get to know you, you're actually pretty great."

He gave me a gentle smile. "So how did you get that from the tree?"

"Well, I guess when you first look at the tree, you notice the twist in the trunk. But once you focus on the other parts, you see that it's actually kind of beautiful."

His smile broadened. "So you think I'm beautiful."

My face flushed with heat. "Now you're just putting words into my mouth." Words that were truer than I'd like to admit.

"Sure I am."

I stepped closer to the tree to get my mind off of what he may or may not be thinking about me right now. I drew in a deep breath and focused on the ornaments he and

Jace had hung on the tree. They weren't the sparkly, expensive kind like the one's I'd seen on the tree we'd passed downstairs. Instead, they all looked very handmade.

"Did you and Jace make all these?" I touched the star that was made out of popsicle sticks.

Logan stepped beside me, so close that our arms brushed. "Yeah, most of them, anyway."

There was a transparent green globe that had a piece of paper with something written on it. "What's that ornament?" I pointed.

Logan shrugged. "My mom thought it would be fun for us to write something we're thankful for every year and put it in one of those."

There were a dozen or more similar globes hanging around the tree. Some were red, green, and some were gold, but they all had slips of paper within.

My gaze caught on the bottom of a gold one with the words *Logan age 16* written on it. It would be the ornament from last year.

I couldn't help but be curious about what he'd been thankful for just a year ago.

It was probably his Corvette. Or possibly his ex-girlfriend. If they'd been dating at that time.

And since the thought had been put in my mind, I just had to know.

I really hoped it didn't say Olivia with stupid red hearts drawn all around it.

"Mind if I look?" I asked, pointing to it.

He got a wary look on his face, but said, "Sure."

I didn't like that look.

He reached up high and got it down for me.

I turned it in my hand so the writing was visible. And I was not expecting the single word written on the paper: *Sobriety.*

Sobriety?

I peered up at Logan with what was sure to be a confused expression. "You're thankful for sobriety?"

He nodded. "Yeah."

"Why?"

I'd never heard of someone my age being thankful for that.

A shadow crossed his face, almost like he was ashamed. He took off his hat and ran his fingers through his hair before replacing it back on his head. "Christmas last year marked my first month of being sober."

I furrowed my brows, still not understanding. "What do you mean?"

He drew in a deep breath and released it slowly. "I'm a recovering alcoholic."

*An alcoholic.*

The words stuck in my mind. I'd heard of people

being called alcoholics before, but in my head they were all middle-aged, angry men who abused their families. They weren't incredibly handsome and vibrant teenage boys. They weren't people like Logan.

"Why do you say you're an alcoholic instead of just someone who liked drinking?"

He turned and went to sit in the corner of the loveseat. "Because I didn't just like it. It was all I cared about for a long time." He gave me a sad look. "And when it gets to the point where all you can think about is where you're going to get your next drink, that kind of tips people off that there might be more to it than simply getting buzzed on the weekends."

"Wow, I had no idea." I went to sit on the cushion next to him.

He nodded to the ornament that I still held in my hand. "Anyway, I wrote that a year ago, after my family held an intervention and sent me to alcoholics anonymous with the threat of rehab if I didn't go."

I looked at the ornament again, turning it in my hands to read the word once more. It was so weird to think that someone my age would be dealing with something like that. Going to AA meetings.

"Have you had anything to drink since you wrote this?" I held the ornament up.

He took it from my hand, his fingers brushing against mine in the exchange. He shook his head. "Not a drop."

"That's amazing."

"Thank you." He looked down, his jaw flexing, and it almost appeared like he was getting a little choked up. "It's been a long road."

We sat there quietly for a time. I didn't really know what to say, but I felt he was okay with the silence.

He put the ornament on the end table beside him. "Anyway, it helps to have reminders of how far I've come."

"Is it still a temptation?"

"Yeah. That's why I have this." He held up his wrist that had a leather bracelet with the words "one day at a time" stamped into it. "And this." He pulled his phone out of his pocket and showed me the lock screen. The photo of the mountain with the same words across it.

"I wondered what that quote was for." I reached over to run my fingers across his bracelet.

He put his phone back in his pocket. "Whenever I start thinking about drinking again, I close my eyes and do some deep breathing to remind myself that I just need to say no to one drink at a time and take this process one day at a time." He draped his arm across the back of the loveseat so his fingers were resting close to my shoulder. "It's been a difficult road, but it's getting easier. As long as I stay busy and stay away from the party scene, I do okay."

"Is that why you left the party so early last week?" I'd assumed it was just because he wanted to leave before I could smack him after finding out he was Logan instead of Jace, but maybe it was because of this.

He nodded. "Yeah. I just came to play a trick on our friends, but then I had to get out of there. But I can't say I'm not happy I did show up. I wouldn't have gotten to kiss you if I hadn't." He winked.

Butterflies erupted in my stomach. I decided to be brave and said, "I'm glad you were there, too."

"Even though I tricked you?"

I nodded. "Yeah."

And I couldn't help but let my gaze fall to his lips. I wanted to kiss him again. His lips were soft and full, and I wanted to taste them.

His fingers grazed along my shoulder. "I think that's the first time I've actually told anyone that story."

"It is?" The words came out breathlessly.

"Yeah." His fingers traced across my shoulder and up my neck, causing goosebumps to raise across my skin. Was he thinking about kissing me, too?

"What about Olivia? Did you tell her?"

He shook his head. "No."

Really? My insides warmed with thoughts of what this could mean. Did Logan really trust me more than he'd trusted her?

Was I really starting to mean something to him like I hoped?

He found a lock of my hair that had fallen from my ponytail and twisted it around his finger. "I've always wanted to touch your hair like this." .

"You have?"

What was he thinking about right now?

He released the lock of hair and brushed the back of his hand against the side of my face. "This too."

"Yeah?" My nerve endings sparked to life as he trailed a finger down my cheek and then across my bottom lip.

I had to bite my lip at the sensation his touch created. My lips were ultra-sensitive.

"Thanks for going ice skating with me today," he said. His finger traced down my chin, and I couldn't help but lean my head against his hand when he caressed my cheek again.

What was he doing?

He was driving me crazy, that's what he was doing.

"We should probably go to the hot tub, huh?" His voice was huskier than usual. "I'm sure Jace and Alyssa will be here soon."

"Hmm?" I asked, my brain unable to focus on what he was saying because it was too distracted by the way he was now trailing his fingers along the back of my ear.

His lips quirked up into a smile at my response. He

totally knew what he was doing to me. And he liked it.

"So you think we should go downstairs?" he asked.

I closed my eyes. He was talking to me, I knew it. But I seriously couldn't form a response because my brain was turning to mush.

I felt him lean closer, so close his warm breath was on my lips when he spoke. "Unless there's something else you'd rather do right now."

His lips were just right there, hovering centimeters above my own. If I pursed my lips, they'd be touching his.

Electricity crackled between us. I wanted to kiss him so badly. Wanted him to kiss me.

But I would wait. I wouldn't make the first move in case I was reading things wrong.

His fingers threaded their way through my long ponytail now. "Your hair is silkier than I imagined," he whispered.

I opened my eyes and looked at him through my lashes. "You've imagined what it would feel like?"

He nodded as his fingers combed through my hair. "Lots of times."

*Lots of times?*

His nose grazed against mine and our breath mingled. We were so close. It made my lungs constrict, and it was a good thing we were sitting down because my legs would have given out on me by now.

"Raven..." He looked at me carefully, his blue eyes pleading in a way as his chest heaved. "Is it—"

"I'll see if they're up here." Jace's voice came from the staircase, cutting through the air and through whatever Logan had been about to say. A second later, Jace appeared at the opening to their room. "Oh, sorry." He looked embarrassed. "Alyssa and I were wondering where you guys were."

"I was just showing Raven our tree." Logan pushed himself away from me, and I didn't miss the look of frustration on his face.

I cleared my throat and sat up straighter. "Yeah, you guys did a great job of decorating it." I forced enthusiasm into my voice, so the boys wouldn't hear how disappointed I was that my moment with Logan had been interrupted.

"Thanks," Jace said, gazing at the tree instead of at Logan or me. "Anyway, I'm just going to change real quick. Alyssa is waiting for us downstairs. We were just about to go to the pool."

Logan stood and looked at me, his expression awkward. "I'll just go change into my swim shorts, too, if you want to wait for me at the bottom of the stairs."

I nodded and stood, my legs still shaky and wobbly from the last few minutes.

Downstairs, Alyssa was waiting for me. She raised her eyebrows. "What were you and Logan doing up there?"

Heat rose to my cheeks. "We were just talking."

She gave me a knowing look. "Sure you were."

"Actually, we were. You guys got back too soon for anything else to happen."

"Sorry about that. But this is good, right? It means that Logan probably likes you, don't you think?"

I glanced up the stairs as I remembered how he had been running his fingers through my hair and along my shoulders and cheeks. "I hope so."

The guys came down a minute later in their swim trunks. And, apparently, Logan hadn't wanted to overwhelm me too much yet, because he still had a T-shirt on.

"The pool's this way," Jace said, leading the way. Alyssa followed behind him while Logan and I walked side by side down the wide hallway to the back of the house. Our hands brushed as we walked, and electricity zipped up my arm.

Jace opened a glass door that led into a large room with lots of windows and a pretty good-sized pool and a hot tub.

"We have two bathrooms over there that you ladies can change in." Jace pointed to the two doors across from us.

I peeked over at Logan. "I guess I'll see you guys in a minute."

He smiled at me. "Can't wait."

## CHAPTER THIRTEEN

ONCE I SHUT the door to the bathroom, I put my hair up into a messy bun. Then I changed into my high-neck blue-and-white striped swimsuit. I tied the strings behind my neck and gave my reflection an inspection.

Deciding that I looked all right, I grabbed my towel out of my bag and then went back to the boys.

Jace was already in the pool when I came out. Logan was sitting on the edge with his feet in the water, like he was waiting for me. I'd always known that the Carmichael twins had won the genetic lottery, but I had to work hard to keep from gasping as I ogled Logan without his shirt on. His chest and arms were tanned, probably from surfing the North Carolina coast all summer. And his body was definitely not the same as it had been when they'd lived here before. He was no longer a gangly teen too long for his body. Logan was full grown now in a man's body. A *very* nice-looking man's body with abs and muscled arms.

I set my towel on the lounge chair next to the pool before walking over and lowering myself to sit beside him.

"Hi," I said.

"Hi." He leaned closer so our shoulders brushed against each other, and when he seemed to take in my appearance, I held my breath. His gaze ran the length of my body before his eyes stopped on my face. A slow smile lifted his lips. "Great swimsuit," he said.

I looked down at my tankini. I'd gotten it last summer when my family went on vacation to the Hamptons to stay at my rich cousin's beach house. I usually bought bikinis, but this one had fit me too perfectly to pass up.

"Thanks."

"Are you ready to get in?" he asked, eyeing the water before looking back at me.

"I think I'll wait for Alyssa." Usually, pools were colder than I liked, but the water felt nice on my legs. Which made sense—fancy people could afford a good heating system.

"Suit yourself." Logan slipped into the water, going all the way in. And when he stood up and ran his hands through his hair to push it out of his eyes, I couldn't help but stare at the way it emphasized his biceps. Logan had been lifting weights since the last time I'd seen him at a pool.

Alyssa came out a minute later, but instead of wearing her swimsuit like I expected, she was wearing her regular clothes and holding up a very scraggly piece of fabric.

"What's that?" I called to her across the pool.

She shook her head. "Apparently, this is my brother's revenge."

And now I could see that it was her swimsuit, except there were a bunch of slits all around it. "Did he attack it with scissors?"

She pursed her lips into a frown. "Yep. I'm officially going to kill him."

Jace had stopped swimming his laps and swam to the end closest to Alyssa. "Caleb did that?"

"Yup. Gotta love that little tormentor of mine." Alyssa sighed. "Anyway, I might as well go home since I can't swim in this."

"We could grab a snack instead of you leaving. I'm actually hungrier than I thought," Jace said, quickly.

She gave him a confused expression but said, "Okay?"

Jace lifted himself out of the pool in one smooth move, and when he stood a few feet from Alyssa, I didn't miss the way she looked at his dripping wet body.

Should Trey be worried?

"How about you guys make us something while you're at it?" Logan called to them.

Jace toweled off and looked back at us. "Sure." And before I knew it, Logan and I were alone again.

"So are you coming in anytime soon?" Logan asked after I continued to sit on the edge of the pool. "The water's nice."

"I don't know. I kind of think the view might be nicer from here." I winked.

A smirk lifted his lips. "The view's not so bad from here, either."

I let my legs swish in the water. "I think I want to just get in the hot tub."

He raised his eyebrow. "And why's that?"

*Because I've always wanted to kiss a guy in a hot tub.*

But I couldn't say that now, could I?

He swam closer. "Well, we have this rule that you have to get cold first before you can get in the hot tub. That way you can really appreciate it."

"Really?" I looked around to see if they had any rules posted on the walls like public pools usually did. "I don't see this so-called rule anywhere."

"That's because it's a secret rule."

I laughed. "Oh, a secret rule."

He nodded. "Only special people get to know about the secret rules."

I grinned. "So, if I get in the pool first, then I can go into the hot tub?"

"Yes." Then he seemed to think of something else. "Unless you want to join the super elite group of awesome people and prove that you are really deserving of the hot tub by completing the top-secret challenge."

"The top-secret challenge?"

His smile broadened. "You have to be pretty amazing to complete this challenge, though."

I felt my competitive nature beginning to rise within me. "I'm up for it."

"Are you sure?"

"Yes."

He looked behind him, and it was then that I noticed a glass door that led to their backyard. Was he going to make me stand outside in the cold for a minute before I could get in the hot tub?

He gave me a sneaky smile. "I dare you to go out there and make a snow angel for five seconds before getting in the hot tub."

"What?" My jaw dropped. "You can't be serious. It's, like, fifteen degrees outside."

He held his hands up at his sides. "If you're not up to the challenge, I get it."

"Oh, I'm up to it." I crossed my arms, feeling myself get all riled up. "The question is if you are."

He laughed. "I most definitely am."

I stood and beckoned for him to join me out of the pool. "Then let's go."

He swam to where I'd been seated a second before, and soon he was towering over me, with droplets of water clinging to his skin and eyelashes.

I decided not to mention that it was going to be way worse for him outside since he was already wet.

He led me toward the back door and put his hand on the knob, glancing back to me before he could turn it. "See that patch of snow right there?" He touched the glass, pointing to a slight hill just a few feet from the door. "That's where we're going."

"Okay." I sighed, my skin already anticipating how cold this was going to be.

"We'll both go out together and you have to lie down in the snow for the full five seconds."

"Got it." My heart was already racing. This was possibly one of the stupidest things I'd ever done, but for some reason, I was excited. Probably because I was doing this with Logan and he made everything more fun.

He drew in a deep breath. "As soon as I open this door, we're going."

I nodded.

And then he opened it. The cool, late December air blew through the open doorway and I immediately ran out into it. I tiptoed onto the snow-covered ground and raced Logan to the hill.

"And down," Logan said, and from the sound in his voice, I could tell how cold he already was.

My skin was already shocked from the brisk wind, the last thing I wanted to do was lie down in the snow. But there was no turning back now.

I plunked down on my butt and yelped.

"Five seconds." Logan called out beside me and we both lay on our backs at the same time. Everything in me told me to jump up and run inside. The snow wasn't supposed to be touching my bare arms, legs, and back like this. I immediately started moving my arms up and down and my legs out and in as Logan counted, "One. Two..."

My body started shivering uncontrollably, but I forced myself to finish.

"Three. Four. Five."

Logan bolted up faster than I'd seen anyone move before, and I chased after him, shaking so badly that I worried I might collapse on the floor. I shut the door behind me and then walked as quickly as I could to the edge of the hot tub.

Normally, I liked to slip into a hot tub slowly, to let my body acclimate to the hot water. But not this time. I practically jumped in the hot tub, head under the water and all.

"You're crazy," I said to Logan when he resurfaced beside me, my teeth chattering as the hot water pulsed around me.

He grinned and wrapped his arms around me, pulling me close to his chest with my arms folded between us. "We did it," he said, his teeth chattering as badly as mine as we stood there together with just our heads above the water.

I continued to shake uncontrollably, my head resting against his neck as I tried to get warm again. "H-have you done that before?"

He rubbed his hands up and down my back. "No."

"Then why did you dare me to do it? I could have gotten hypothermia." I smacked his chest gently.

He chuckled, a low rumble against my ear. "You can't get hypothermia from five seconds in the snow."

I wanted to argue but decided not to. My shivering eventually stopped as we stood there huddled together. And once we were both still and I wasn't so focused on how bad I was shaking anymore, I was suddenly aware of just how close we were—I was huddled up to Logan's bare chest in a hot tub. His very nice masculine chest.

I let my fingers trace the water droplets clinging to his clavicle. Let my fingers run over the muscles in his shoulders and upper arms.

I'd never been this close to a guy who wasn't wearing a shirt before.

I was just looking at his shoulders in a distracted and awed sort of way when he cleared his throat, bringing me back to my senses.

And when I looked up to him, there was something in his eyes that made my stomach muscles tighten.

"Hi," he said.

"Hey," I said.

And before I could think of anything else to say, his lips were on mine. There was nothing tentative about it, either—he just full-on kissed me. We'd only kissed each other once before, but the instant our lips touched, it was like they picked right up from where they'd left off under the mistletoe. His arms tightened around my waist, and he gently pulled me with him as he took a seat along the hot tub's wall, setting me down beside him.

"Is this okay?" Logan broke away for a second, sounding as out of breath as I felt.

My shoulders heaved as I tried to catch my breath. "More than okay." And then I pressed my lips against his again, this time deepening the kiss. I let my hands move from where they rested behind his neck and slipped them into his wet hair, pulling myself even closer.

His hands slid up my back and pressed me tight

against his chest so there was no space between our bodies anymore.

"Remember how I said legendary might be too big of a word to describe your kissing skills?" Logan mumbled after a while.

"Yeah?" I asked, my mind not really all there as our lips locked.

"I don't think legendary was the right word."

I froze. "It's not?"

He shook his head. "I think you need a bigger word."

My heart did a cartwheel in my chest. "Do you have a new word in mind?"

He shook his head. "I can't—" He trailed kisses along my jaw, making a path of fire follow everywhere his lips touched. "—really—" His lips traveled back toward my mouth. "—think right now." And when our mouths touched again, I had the feeling that we just might ignite if we weren't already doused in water.

His hands smoothed their way up my back and down again until they tightened against my waist and he pulled me onto his lap. I gasped in surprise, but then I relaxed against him a moment later, letting my hands slide out of his hair and rest behind his neck to steady myself against him.

We kissed for a while longer before I heard the door behind us open.

I pulled away—needing the moment to catch my breath, anyway—and then turned to look, just in time to see the glass door closing again and Jace walking away.

"My brother is really good at catching us really close together," Logan said, his voice huskier than usual.

I turned back to him with a smile on my lips. "He probably came to tell us our snack was ready."

Logan stared at my lips then met my eyes again, his pupils bigger than usual. "Little does he know I just tasted something better than he and Alyssa could ever whip up in the kitchen."

I pressed my swollen lips together. "Me, too."

"We should probably go, though." His fingertips ran across the small of my back where my tankini had slipped up a little. "If my mom finds out I was kissing you in the hot tub, I'll be banned."

My heart pounded. "Why?" I pushed myself off his lap and straightened my swimsuit at the mention of his mom finding us.

"One of our pool rules. No kissing gorgeous girls in the pool or hot tub."

I grinned. "Is that another one of your secret rules?"

"I wish." He leaned closer, making my stomach muscles tighten again with anticipation. "'Cuz I wouldn't hesitate breaking it again if it was." He looked at my lips one more time, and I thought for a moment that he was going to kiss me again until he stood. "But I'm going to be a good boy now."

My heart sank a little. Was it bad that I really wanted him to have a streak of bad boy left in him?

He stepped out of the hot tub a moment later, and I followed him. We both toweled off, and I tried not to stare too long at his chest muscles as he ran his towel along his arms. Had I really just been kissing him in the hot tub?

It almost didn't seem real.

"Ready?" he asked once we were dried off and I'd put my coverup over my swimsuit.

"Sure."

## CHAPTER FOURTEEN

"DID something happen between you and Logan in the pool?" Alyssa asked when she drove me home later that afternoon. We'd gotten a snack and then watched the movie *Elf* in the Carmichael's theater room. And while Logan and I hadn't come out and told Jace and Alyssa that we'd just made-out in the hot tub, we hadn't necessarily been discreet that there were sparks flying between us with all the longing looks we'd given each other.

I fiddled with the zipper on my coat, trying to decide if I wanted to tell her. I was pretty sure Logan liked me—he seemed to enjoy kissing me, at least. But would it totally jinx everything if I told her? It seemed like every time I told her I'd kissed a guy, he'd turned around the next day and kissed someone else.

But Alyssa had said she was going to watch us today,

so maybe she'd be able to guide me. "We kind of kissed in the hot tub."

She glanced at me as she drove, her eyes wide. "You guys kissed?"

I nodded, unable to keep a small smile from taking shape on my face. "And it was really good."

She smiled. "From the look on your face, I'd assumed as much."

I laughed. "Yeah. I know we always daydreamed of what it would be like to kiss a Carmichael, but my imagination had nothing on what Logan's lips can really do to a girl."

"You guys just kissed, right?"

I whacked her arm. "Of course!"

She shrugged. "Just making sure. Hot tub kisses do have a reputation for a reason."

Now it was my turn to look shocked. "I may be Rebound Raven, but I'm not that big of a rebound."

She looked at me. "You don't think you're his rebound, do you?"

"I hope not." But now that the thought was in my head, I couldn't get it out. Logan had just gotten out of a relationship recently. And he had told me I wasn't supposed to fall in love with him or anything when we first started hanging out. "Do you think it's a rebound?"

She gave me a look I didn't like. "I'm just worried."

Oh no. Alyssa knew something. "What do you know?"

She shrugged. "When you guys left the rink, I asked Jace why Logan had been so mad, and he told me that Logan's ex-girlfriend was coming to their house for dinner on Friday."

My throat tightened. "And?" I'd known about Olivia coming, but did Alyssa know something that I didn't?

She slid her hands along the steering wheel. "Jace said Logan never wanted to break up with her in the first place."

"So you think he's going to try to get back with her this weekend?" I felt sick. Was I really just a placeholder until the girl he really wanted came back around?

Alyssa must have heard my heart breaking or something, because she hurried to say, "I don't know if he likes her or anything. I really have no idea. I just want you to be careful since I know how things have gone for you in the past. I don't want to see you get hurt again."

I nodded, suddenly feeling the urge to cry.

She touched my arm. "I'm sure everything's fine. Jace was probably just being overly worried since he's like that."

When I still didn't say anything, Alyssa added, "And I bet you're way hotter and funnier than Olivia. Just pretend I didn't say anything."

"I'll try."

Though I had a feeling I'd be obsessing about it until Olivia had come and gone.

Why did all the amazing guys always have to have so many girls to choose from?

---

THE NEXT WEEK was super busy with all the basketball games I had to cheer at, as well as getting all the assignments and tests done before Christmas break started. I still saw Logan during English, and he was still the nice charming version of himself that I'd gotten to know on the weekends. But as the days went on and he didn't say anything about the kiss, or try to hang out again, I started to worry that I'd read things wrong once again. Had the hot tub kiss just been something fun that happened in the moment? If it had been more than a rebound, he'd try to hang out with me again soon, right?

By Friday I was starting to feel a little crazy as thoughts swirled through my mind about how he might turn out to be like every other guy I'd ever liked and go with the other girl in his life.

I was doodling in my notebook before English when Logan took his regular seat in front of me. A whiff of his sigh-inducing cologne met my nostrils, and I couldn't help but have a flashback to when I'd first smelled his scent under the mistletoe as we'd kissed two weeks earlier.

Maybe that was the solution to my problem. Maybe I just needed to find some mistletoe and get him to kiss me, so he could see that the sparks between us were real.

He turned to me with a tentative smile on his face. "Do you have to cheer at an away game tonight?"

I set my pen down on my desk. "No. It's Christmas break so they don't have one."

"Do you have any plans for the weekend then?"

Had he forgotten about the dance tomorrow?

My eyebrows knit together. "Just the Christmas Ball. We're still going together, right?"

"Of course." He gave me a reassuring smile. "What I was trying to ask is whether you have any plans for tonight?"

Relief flowed through me and I let a smile lift my lips. "Alyssa and I were maybe going to a party, but it's not really set in stone yet." In other words: if he wanted to hang out with me after his family's dinner, I could totally cancel my plans.

He looked down at the floor and swallowed before looking back at me. "Would you maybe want to come to my family's dinner party tonight?"

Oh, I hadn't been expecting that.

"You mean the dinner that your ex-girlfriend is going to be at?"

He gave me a cautious look. "That would be the one."

I cast my gaze down at my notebook. "Would it be weird to have me there with your ex-girlfriend?" I mean, unless he really didn't like me and he was just planning to introduce her to all his new buddies.

My chest fell with the thought. I really hoped I wasn't on the verge of being friend-zoned.

"No, I don't think it would be weird at all." He scratched the back of his neck. "Actually, I was kind of hoping you'd come so I could show her that I've moved on."

And there it was. What I'd been worried about all along.

I really was just a rebound girl again.

I worked hard to keep my expression from falling. I'd known going into this that we were just going to the dance together because it was mutually beneficial. He'd never said he liked me, and he had told me I wasn't supposed to fall for him.

I knew I should probably say no and hold onto any sense of self-preservation that I had hiding somewhere inside of me, but I found my mouth saying, "Sure. I can come."

His smile broadened before I could take the words back. "Great. How about I pick you up at six?"

I sighed, my chest caving in on itself. "That'll be great."

Before he turned to face forward, he said, "Oh, and it's a suit-and-tie thing, so if you have an old prom dress or something, that would be a good thing to wear."

Wow. They dressed up for dinner? Maybe I really didn't belong in his world after all.

"I can get a dress," I said.

And I would look fabulous.

I'd allow myself to enjoy this weekend and I'd face reality next week.

## CHAPTER FIFTEEN

FRIDAY AFTERNOON, Alyssa helped me get ready for the dinner party.

"I bet Logan dies when he sees you. You look gorgeous," she said as she curled my hair with my curling iron.

We'd decided I should wear my hair down, in long flowing waves, since it seemed like Logan had a thing for hair.

I swiped mascara across my eyelashes. "I hope he likes it. I can only imagine how hot Olivia is. A guy like Logan could get any girl he wanted."

"You're not exactly a hag, Raven." Alyssa rolled her eyes. "I'd give anything to have your dark complexion and hair." I could tell she was trying to be ultra-upbeat because she felt guilty about putting doubts in my mind in the first place. So I was trying to go along with it for her sake.

I looked at my reflection. I knew I was pretty, but it just seemed like with my luck I must not be pretty enough.

Unless it was something else.

Was I just not nice enough? I'd been pretty mean to Lexi Stevens when she started dating Noah. Was karma keeping me from getting what I wanted? My mom was always telling me that when we put something into the universe, we can't help but be affected by it...

I sighed. "Maybe I need to be nicer. Maybe that's it. Maybe Olivia is really a super, generous, compassionate person." I mean, Logan had volunteered to help with the Winter Wonderland thing while I'd only gone because I'd been forced into it by my mother. Maybe he wanted someone who thought more about other people instead of themselves.

"You're nice, too." Alyssa wrapped some of my hair around the curling iron, and I just cocked an eyebrow and stared at her until she snickered. "Okay, so maybe you can be a little rude sometimes, but you're getting better. And they do say that the first step to recovery is admitting that there's a problem." She grinned.

I laughed and picked up my blush brush. "At least I'm on my way then."

I finished with my makeup and Alyssa finished with my hair a few minutes later. Then I put on the dress I'd worn to prom last spring. It was a gray, off-the-shoulder dress with a long, full skirt with layers and layers of tulle.

When I looked at my reflection in the mirror, I couldn't help but smile. The last time I'd worn this dress, I'd been going to Prom with a guy who'd shown up drunk when he picked me up, and then when we were only about halfway through the night, he'd tried to lure me into a hotel room.

Sadly, most of my formal dances had gone similarly.

This dress deserved a second chance, just like the girl wearing it deserved a chance to land the right twin. I had no idea where Logan was with his feelings these days, but I was determined not to go down without a fight.

---

A FEW MINUTES LATER, my mom called my name from the bottom of the stairs. I looked at my reflection in the mirror once more.

*"You can do this, Raven,"* I whispered to myself. I could make a guy see that I was worth putting some effort into. I was worth Logan seeing me for what I was. Someone like him. Perhaps a little rough around the edges, but someone he clicked with.

I lifted my skirt high enough that I wouldn't trip on it as I went down the stairs. When I turned a corner, I saw him. He was wearing a gray suit with a silky navy-blue tie. But then my gaze went to his hair and I stopped. His hair was combed neatly, just the way it had been two weeks ago under the mistletoe. The same way Jace wore it.

Had Logan decided to send his brother?

"Jace?" I asked, trying not to let my disappointment show too much on my face.

The Carmichael twin, whose identity I wasn't sure of, gave me a wary look before saying, "No. It's Logan." Then he furrowed his brow. "Were you hoping it was Jace?"

"No, of course not." I hurried down the stairs. The last thing I needed was for Logan to think I was still hung up on his brother. He'd already been way too worried about that happening in the past. I stopped in front of him and pointed to his hair. "I just know Jace combs his hair like that and Logan only does when he's pretending to be Jace."

Relief showed on his face. "Oh. Okay."

I bit my lip as I looked at him. He still looked just like Jace. "Are you really Logan?"

His lips lifted into a teasing smile. "Can you really still not tell us apart?"

I shrugged. "Usually the hair and the hat clue me in." I

sighed. "I haven't watched you two together enough recently to see the little differences yet."

How could I expect Logan to tell me he liked me when I couldn't even tell him apart from his brother?

And since I was pathetic, I had to ask, "At the risk of sounding pathetic, can you tell me what I ordered you when you took me to Cafe Amore so I know for sure that you're Logan?"

He smirked, and I saw some of what could only be Logan shining through. "If you must test me, then you ordered me the most delicious French dip sandwich along with a berry salad that changed my life."

I sighed with relief and smiled. It was Logan. "Thanks for clearing that up."

"No problem."

Then he seemed to look me over. I noticed the way his gaze lingered on my hair and I was happy that I'd decided to wear it down.

His expression softened, and it made my stomach muscles tighten. "You look beautiful tonight, by the way."

I dipped my head down as nerves crept over me. "Thank you."

Then it was my turn to take in his appearance. His gray suit looked amazing on him. "You don't look so bad yourself." My fingers itched to run through his hair and put it back the way it normally was. He looked good like this. But I liked his "Logan" look better than his "Jace" look. "I do kind of miss your messy hair, though."

He shrugged. "I look like Jace like this, so you should be happy." He said it lightly, like he was joking, but I couldn't help but wonder if there was a part of him that still thought I might prefer Jace.

Was that why he hadn't invited me to hang out until today? Maybe he had been waiting for me to make the next move, but when I didn't, he'd decided to make his ex-girlfriend jealous instead.

He looked at his watch. "Anyway, we better get going. Dinner starts at six-thirty."

I followed him out the door, and as I walked beside him, not holding his hand like I ached to do, I couldn't help but think that we needed to have a conversation about how I felt about him and how he felt about me soon.

I just hoped that when he saw Olivia again tonight, it wouldn't be too late.

---

"OKAY, so do you remember the plan for tonight?" Logan stopped me in the garage right before we went inside the house. "You're going to pretend to be my girlfriend, just like I pretended for you last week with Noah."

I swallowed. "Right."

He studied my eyes. "You sure you can do it?"

"Of course." I wanted him to call me his girlfriend for real, but I could pretend to be his fake girlfriend.

He held his hand out to me. "Then let's do this."

I intertwined my fingers with his and let him pull me into the house.

Logan led me into his family's formal dining room. There was a long rectangular table, polished dark wood, in the middle with low hanging chandeliers above it. Everyone was already seated at the table when we walked in: his dad, his mom, Jace, and four other people I hadn't seen before who I assumed were Olivia's family. And right next to the two empty chairs was a blonde in a champagne-colored dress.

Olivia.

"Sorry we're late," Logan said, pulling me farther into the room. And when Olivia saw our hands linked together, her expression turned sour. She smoothed the look up into a smile a moment later, but I'd seen it. And I would hold it in my mind. I had a feeling I might need to remember it tonight. Because just like I'd feared, Olivia was gorgeous.

"You're not late," Mr. Carmichael said with a twinkle in his eyes. "We simply sat down early."

Logan pulled out the empty chair beside Jace for me

to sit in, and then he took the one beside me. Which, to my dismay, was also beside Olivia.

*She'd better not try anything funny under the table.*

A few people in white button-up shirts and black pants walked into the room carrying plates of food. As they set them in front of the dinner guests, I heard Olivia say to Logan, "I was worried you heard I was coming and that you decided not to show up." Her voice was lower pitched than I'd expected. When I'd imagined her speaking, it had always been in a much more shrill-sounding voice in my head.

"I'd never dream of missing dinner with your family." Logan lifted his napkin from the table and set it on his lap. "I just ran into traffic when I went to pick up Raven." He turned to me and leaned back so Olivia could see me. "This is Raven, by the way."

"Raven?" Olivia pasted a fake smile onto her face as the server set her plate in front of her. "Nice to meet you."

"Nice to meet you, too," I replied, hoping my words didn't come out as fake-sounding as hers had.

Olivia looked back to Logan. "So, are you two old friends?"

Logan reached over and took my hand in his, linking our fingers together and resting our hands on his thigh. "Raven and I were neighbors growing up, but I was lucky enough to convince her to be my girlfriend shortly after we moved back." He squeezed my hand like he wanted me to say something to follow up.

I cleared my throat. "Yeah, Logan and I go way back. But when he kissed me under the mistletoe that first night back, all my old feelings for him came rushing back." I just wouldn't mention that those feelings had mostly been annoyance and frustration over having been tricked.

Olivia's eyes widened. "He kissed you his first night back?"

I nodded and gave Logan my most loving look. "Yeah. It was the best first kiss I've ever had."

He looked at me, and I'd expected a smirk from him since we were just playing along, but instead, he gave me a questioning one. "Your best first kiss?"

I nodded and forced myself to maintain eye contact. It was risky to let him know just how much my feelings had changed and grown for him. But I couldn't expect amazing things to happen if I didn't put myself out there. I squeezed his hand. "It was."

A slow smiled lifted his lips, and he surprised me by kissing the top of my head quickly. "It was my best first kiss, too."

DINNER WAS delicious despite having Olivia glaring at me all night. But once dessert was served, I was relieved to excuse myself to go to the bathroom.

All throughout dinner, Logan had been super sweet and attentive. He held my hand, sometimes placing his on my thigh in a romantic gesture. Basically, he was acting like the boyfriend I'd always wanted, and it was so hard not knowing if there was any truth behind what he was doing. Or if it was all just a show for Olivia.

He'd said he wanted to show her that he'd moved on, but I think my brain was wanting so badly for it to be real that it was inventing the little soft looks and the reasons for why he kept bumping against me and touching me.

Was it completely stupid of me to hope there were real feelings mixed in there somewhere?

I looked in the mirror and tried to tell myself that it didn't matter. That I would be okay if it turned out to be exactly what Logan had talked about this morning. I had pretty much hated him two weeks ago. I would be totally fine if he decided to rekindle things with Olivia.

But I knew I was just lying to myself.

I wanted him.

If I was one of those little kids sitting on Santa's lap and telling him what I wanted for Christmas, I knew exactly what I'd ask for. I'd ask for Logan. For Logan Carmichael to be mine and for me to be his. That was what I wanted Santa to bring me this year. Not just a weekend of fun with Logan, but as much time as I could get.

So I knew what I needed to do. I needed to tell him how I felt. I needed to be brave and put myself out there. I needed to risk getting my heart broken again, because if I didn't, I'd be no better off than I was now. At least if I told him how I felt, he'd know, and then maybe he'd tell me his feelings. Good or bad. I needed to know so I could stop making myself crazy.

So I dried my hands on one of their fancy towels, remembering how kindly Logan had treated me the first time I came to their house. He'd bandaged me up. He'd taken care of me. He'd treated me like no other guy had treated me before.

This could work. Maybe things would go my way for once. I would finally get the guy—maybe not the guy I'd thought I always wanted—but the guy who was so unbelievably perfect for me it was crazy I hadn't figured it out sooner.

I switched off the light and walked out into the hall. But when I turned the corner, I tripped on my dress, because there, against the wall, just fifteen feet away was Logan with his back to me, kissing Olivia with such fierceness I felt like I might need to wash my eyes with holy water based on how hot the passion between them was.

I'd thought our hot tub kiss had been good, but it had nothing on this.

I covered my mouth with my hand as a sob like I'd never heard before, ripped out of me.

He'd picked her. Just like every other guy I'd ever wanted. He'd picked the *other* girl.

## CHAPTER SIXTEEN

I NEEDED to get out of here. I didn't need to just stand here watching Logan kiss Olivia. The longer I looked, the more firmly it would be burned into my mind, and I wanted it out. I wanted it all out.

I'd been wrong. Knowing how he really felt about me was much worse than wondering. Much, much worse. I'd rather not have known, because this—watching his obvious lack of feelings for me and abundance of feelings for his ex—was more than I could take.

And I most definitely didn't need to be standing here when he and Olivia finally came up for air.

So I turned to head back the way I'd come. I'd never been through the Carmichael's front door since I'd always come through the garage, but the front of their house had to be here somewhere.

I walked down one hall, trying to keep my heels from clacking too loudly on the floor and alerting Logan to the fact that I'd caught him.

After coming to a dead end filled with closed doors instead of a front room, I turned around again and went in search of another outlet.

I made it back to the hall where Logan and Olivia were still kissing. I slipped around the corner as quietly as I could into another corridor, only looking back once I was a safe distance away just to make sure they hadn't noticed me sneak past. Logan's fingers were tangled in Olivia's hair now, and I felt my heart rip apart in my chest. He was supposed to be doing that with *my* hair tonight.

I turned away from them to watch where I was going. The clanking of dishes sounded lightly in my ears, and I sighed with relief. It may not be the front door, but I knew there was a back exit I could sneak out this way. I could just tell Pam to let Logan know that I'd decided to walk home.

In the freezing December air.

And without a coat, because I hadn't needed one in Logan's Corvette on the way here.

The kitchen was just coming in view when someone came from another hall and sideswiped me.

"Sorry," the deep voice said, sounding just as startled as I was.

I kept my head down. It was Jace. I couldn't let him see that I was crying. He'd just go and tell Logan.

But instead of letting me walk past him and let me keep some of my dignity still intact, he put his hands on my shoulders and stopped me.

"Hey, what's wrong?" he asked in a gentle voice.

I kept my eyes down, looking at his blue tie. "I'm leaving."

He touched my chin and lifted it, so I was forced to look at him—look into the eyes that were identical to his brother's.

"Why are you leaving? What's wrong?"

My shoulders drooped, and I felt another sob rising in me. I knew I was going to burst into tears and make a complete fool of myself, so I drew in a shaky breath as a last-ditch effort to keep everything in control. He touched my cheek and said, "Raven, you're worrying me." The sound of his voice, which was the same as his brother's, had me falling apart.

I sniffled and wiped my eyes. "I just saw Logan making out with Olivia."

He furrowed his brows. "What? Where?"

I pointed behind me in their general direction. "In the hall by the bathroom." The bathroom where Logan had taken such good care of me the first time I'd been to this house.

I pinched my eyes shut. I knew I was going to look like a disaster. I'd worn waterproof mascara, but it could only hold up so well.

Jace wiped at the tears under my eyes. "Please don't cry, Raven."

"But I..." I shook my head. "It wasn't supposed to be this way. He was supposed to pick me."

He wiped at the tears beneath my other eye and gave me the most understanding look I'd ever seen. "But he did choose you, Raven."

I snorted. "He's kissing Olivia. He just wanted me to help him make her jealous, so he could get a nice, hot make-out sesh before she went back to North Carolina."

Jace ran a hand through his hair and messed it up. "But Raven, you're not seeing things right. That's not me back there. You must have seen Jace."

I shook my head. "You don't need to try to cover for your brother, Jace. I know it's him. Why in the world would you be kissing Olivia?"

"Probably because Jace is frustrated that your best friend is dating Trey, and guys sometimes do stupid things to blow off steam."

"What?"

The guy in front of me, who I was growing less certain of who he actually was, nodded. "I'm Logan." He stepped closer and put both his hands on either side of my face.

"Go ahead and test me. Ask me another question like you did when I picked you up."

"Logan?" I felt lightheaded. "Is that really you?"

He smiled his signature smile that I'd grown to love and pulled the sleeve back on his suit coat to reveal a leather bracelet with the words *one day at a time* stamped in it. "It's me."

"So you're not kissing Olivia right now?"

"No." He shook his head.

"But I thought...?"

And this time I looked at his eyes. Really looked at his eyes, and my heart banged against my ribcage when I saw that he was looking at me in the exact way that I'd been dreaming about all week.

He let his fingers trace along my cheek until it slipped behind my neck, and then he wound a lock of my hair around his finger. "Why would I be kissing Olivia when the only thing I've thought about all week is finding the right moment to kiss you again?"

And before I knew what was happening, he pulled me closer and pressed his lips to mine. I went still, my brain needing a moment to catch up to what was happening.

"Just kiss me, Raven," Logan said when I still wasn't responding. "Kiss me the way I've been dying for you to kiss me all week."

My heart squeezed in my chest. "You really wanted this all week?"

"Way longer than that, actually."

And when he kissed me again, this time I was ready. I pressed myself onto my tiptoes and slipped my hands up his chest. His heart beat strong and fast, almost as fast as mine, and I knew he really did want this as much as I did. I slipped my arms behind his neck. He was tall and strong, and when he wrapped his arms behind my waist, pulling me so close there was no space left between us, I couldn't help but let my walls crumble down.

My lips melded with his, fitting together in a way I'd never experienced before. I'd kissed him twice before, but those kisses had nothing on this. Because this time I had the promise of him liking me back.

His hands smoothed their way up my spine. Up the laces of my dress that I now realized I may have tied too tight, because being this close to Logan and kissing him this way was making it hard to breathe. His hands moved in slow circles, making my brain foggy, and my stomach muscles tightened and twisted.

"We should have been doing this every day since I moved back," Logan mumbled against my lips before he moved to kiss my jaw, my neck, my ear.

I pulled myself even closer to him, needing him to hold me up because my legs were no longer strong enough to hold me. He responded by pushing my back against the wall and pressing himself against me until our bodies were flushed with one another.

He kissed the curve of my neck. Trailed kisses along my shoulder. My skin burned everywhere his lips touched. And it was all I could do to draw in a decent breath as he made me feel things I'd never felt before. I'd kissed my fair share of guys, but I had never experienced a kiss like this. One that brought me to life, lit me on fire, and made me never want to ever do anything besides kiss Logan for the rest of my life.

His lips found mine again and he deepened the kiss, threading his fingers into my hair at the same time. Chills coursed through my body with how amazing it felt.

"Sorry I'm messing up your hair," he said, breaking away after a while.

I shook my head. "I don't mind."

But he started smoothing my hair down anyway, his chest heaving as if he was having a hard time catching his breath.

I just watched him as he carefully tried to make me look more presentable.

When he was done, he inspected me. "We can't have both of us going around with messy hair, now can we?"

It wasn't necessarily funny, but I was so giddy right

then that I giggled. Yes, *giggled*—like a middle schooler watching her crush walk by.

He drew in a deep breath and leaned his forehead against mine, our eyes locking. "So, in case you didn't understand from what just happened, I kind of really like you Raven Rodgers."

"Yeah?"

He nodded his head emphatically. "I've kind of had a crush on you for a long time."

"You have?"

"Yes."

"Then why did you tell me two weeks ago that I wasn't allowed to fall for you because you weren't ready for a relationship?" I asked, confused.

"I said that to protect myself."

"What do you mean?"

He gave me a smile that warmed my whole insides and made my knees weak. "How could you not know that I've always had a crush on you?"

My heart thumped in my chest. "You had a crush on me?"

He nodded as he ran his hands across my shoulders. "I only noticed how much you spied on me and my brother because I was trying to get a glance at you."

"But..." I blinked my eyes, not believing him.

He took my face in his hands and leaned his forehead

against mine. "You don't have to worry about being the rebound girl with me, Raven, because you're *the* girl. You've always been the girl."

My heart swelled in my chest. Could I even hope that it was true?

I studied his eyes for a sign or a hint that he was just joking around with me like he'd been the first time we'd kissed, but there was nothing but truth in his eyes. And adoration.

"I like you too, Logan. So much."

Our lips met in a long, slow exchange, and this time I knew that he wanted this as much as I did. He actually cared about me. And the thought that Logan Carmichael, the guy who I'd thought was my enemy all these years, could actually like me as much as I liked him boggled my mind. I'd always thought we were like repelling magnets, both of us turned the wrong way, always pushing to get away from one another. But it turned out all we needed was to understand each other and be open to letting down the walls, so we could fit together perfectly.

I don't know how long we stood kissing in the hall, but when we eventually broke apart, Logan took my hand and led me away so he could take me home.

"You know," he said with a half-smile on his lips. "It *was* kind of nice seeing you get so jealous and emotional over me."

My jaw dropped. "You like it when girls cry over you, Logan?"

"No." He gave me a rueful smile. "But I like knowing that you care." He squeezed my hand.

I squeezed his hand back. "Well, as long as you don't make a habit of enjoying seeing me cry, I guess I can give you a pass."

## CHAPTER SEVENTEEN

LOGAN PICKED me up first thing the next morning so we could spend the day together before the dance that night. And it was a good thing he'd shown up so early, because once noon hit, the snow was falling like crazy and we were snowed in for the afternoon.

"You sure you still want to go to the Christmas Ball in weather like this?" Logan looked out the window as we fixed ourselves some hot chocolate in his kitchen.

I looked out the window, too. The snow was so thick and falling so fast I could only see a few feet out his window before everything was just white.

I raised an eyebrow. "What do you think?"

He shrugged. "I really don't know, that's kind of why I'm asking."

I just stared at him like he was saying crazy stuff. "Of course I want to go. There's no way I'm not showing up after the way Emily suggested I could sit at the singles table."

Logan held his hands up and laughed. "Got it. I get to wear my suit two nights in a row."

"You got that right." Then I remembered something. "Just make sure to do your hair the right way tonight, okay?"

He grinned and ran his fingers through his hair, pushing it to the side in the messy way that I loved. "Like this?"

I laughed. "Yes. Just like that."

I lifted my mug from the counter and tried a sip. My mouth instantly burned, and I yelped, "Hot!"

Logan turned to me with a smirk. "Thank you."

It took me a moment to realize why he was thanking me, and once I did, I couldn't help but roll my eyes. "I was calling my hot chocolate hot. Not you."

He raised his eyebrows and leaned closer. "But you still think I'm hot, right?"

"Duh."

He laughed and blew into his mug as he stepped back from the counter. "Let's go into the living room to watch the snow by the fire."

Now if that didn't sound like the perfect way to spend the Saturday before Christmas, I didn't know what did.

Logan took the corner of the couch and I sat right beside him, loving that I could do this. We hadn't necessarily come out and said what we were to each other, but with everything that had happened last night, I hoped we weren't too far off from boyfriend and girlfriend.

Logan grabbed a remote from a compartment in the armrest beside him and pressed a button to light the gas fireplace. Then he grabbed another remote and switched on the white twinkling lights on their huge Christmas tree nearby.

"That's nice," I said.

Logan smiled. "You know what would make it nicer?"

I frowned, not able to guess.

He continued when I didn't say anything, "It would be nicer if my girlfriend was cuddled up to me on the couch."

I couldn't keep a smile off my face. "Your girlfriend?"

He shrugged and set his mug on the coffee table. "Well, that is if you want to be called my girlfriend."

"I think that might be okay." I set my mug next to his and snuggled closer to him, resting my head on his shoulder. "But only with one condition."

He pulled me closer and rubbed his hand across my arm. "And what's that?"

"I get to call you my boyfriend."

I looked up and watched his lips spread into a grin. "I think I can handle that."

He bent closer and kissed me softly and slowly for a moment. When we broke apart, he sighed and squeezed me closer. "Yeah, I think I'm going to like being your boyfriend. A lot."

I couldn't agree more. I'd always wanted a boyfriend and it looked like I'd gotten my Christmas wish a little early this year.

We sat there cuddling for a moment before I decided my hot chocolate was probably cool enough to drink. I lifted my mug to my mouth and took a sip. This time, the creamy, chocolatey goodness was just the right temperature.

"So, does Jace know that we know about him kissing Olivia?" I asked.

Logan grinned. "Yup."

"And?" That smile had to mean something.

"He was pretty humiliated when I told him that you saw them."

I laughed. "Then why did he do it?"

Logan got a contemplative look on his face as he blew into his mug and stirred his hot chocolate with a candy cane. "Did Alyssa ever tell you what happened the night before we moved away?"

I tried to conjure memories of that day, but all I remembered was watching his family load up their moving van.

"I don't remember anything special. Just that I was sad that you guys were moving."

"Sad that Jace was moving away." He nudged me playfully with his elbow. "You were probably doing cartwheels all around your front yard at the thought of me being gone."

"Did you have a hidden camera somewhere to spy on my reaction after you left?"

Logan's jaw dropped, and he put a hand to his chest. "Cartwheels? Really?"

I laughed. "I was in gymnastics, of course I was doing cartwheels. I probably threw in a few back handsprings, too."

He shook his head. "You're ruthless, you know that?"

I shrugged. "I was young and didn't have as good of taste in twins as I do now."

"Luckily I found a mistletoe to help us get things right, huh?"

"Yes, thank goodness for mistletoes." I set my mug back on the coffee table then turned back to Logan, tucking my feet beneath me. "But all joking aside, what does Alyssa have anything to do with why Jace was kissing Olivia?"

"Promise you won't say anything to Alyssa?" he asked.

I pressed my lips together as I tried to decide whether to agree to what he was saying or not.

"Is it something bad?"

He looked down at his mug. "Not exactly."

"Okay, what is it then?"

"Jace and Alyssa kissed before we left."

"They *what?*" My voice came out too loud. I looked around to make sure Jace wasn't anywhere near. "How did I never know this?"

Logan shrugged. "I guess she probably didn't want to say anything since you still liked my brother."

How could she keep that a secret from me? In the year and a half since then, she hadn't breathed a word of it to me. As far as I'd always thought, Trey had been her first kiss.

"Are you mad?" Logan had a worried expression.

"I'm not exactly happy about it."

"Because you're mad that Jace chose her?"

I shook my head and took Logan's hand. Was he still insecure about that? After everything last night?

I squeezed his hand. "I don't care about who Jace may or may not have chosen. I'm just wondering why she didn't tell me."

"So you're saying you wouldn't dump me if my

brother walked in here and offered to kiss you like he kissed Olivia?"

I rolled my eyes. "Why would I want to kiss him when I already get to call my favorite Carmichael twin my boyfriend?"

*Boyfriend.* I still couldn't believe I actually had one of those now. For so many years I had been known as Rebound Raven. Was it possible that I'd finally been able to retire that title?

Logan kissed me on the forehead. "Well, that's good to hear," he said. "Because I, for one, am excited to see you in your dress tonight and show you my awesome dance skills."

"You have dance skills?" I knew Logan was just full of surprises lately, but I couldn't imagine him dancing.

"Okay, so I pretty much just step from side to side, but I'm okay with you teaching me some of yours tonight."

I smiled. "I think I'm okay with that."

He leaned back against the couch again and gestured for me to cuddle up to him. "You know there is one thing I'm really hoping they have at the dance tonight."

"And what's that?" I scooted close again, resting my head against his chest.

"Mistletoe."

A small smile slipped up on my lips. "But mistletoes can be dangerous, you know."

He kissed me on the forehead. "Only when you're kissing the wrong person. Luckily for us, your mistletoe mix-up was the best thing that could have happened to me."

"The best thing?" I looked up at him with raised eyebrows.

He shrugged. "That and your terrible sixth sense."

---

WANT MORE RAVEN AND LOGAN? Grab your special bonus chapters here: https://BookHip.com/HPGBFMB

---

Read Jace and Alyssa's story next!

*Her crush is back. Too bad he's off-limits.*
Grab it today!

## WANT A FREE BOOK? SIGN UP!

I hope you enjoyed MY MISTLETOE MIX-UP! If you haven't already, please sign up for my newsletter so you can stay up to date on my latest book news. Plus, you'll get two FREE books by me, just for signing up! https://subscribepage.com/judycorry

Join the Corry Crew on Facebook: https://www.facebook.com/groups/judycorrycrew/

Follow me on Instagram: @judycorry

Don't miss the first book in the Eden Falls Academy series.

**My math tutor has one rule: he doesn't date the girls he tutors at our private school. But a fake relationship that's mutually beneficial? That's a different story.**

Grab your copy!

Also By Judy Corry

**Ridgewater High Series:**

When We Began (Cassie and Liam)

Meet Me There (Ashlyn and Luke)

Don't Forget Me (Eliana and Jess)

It Was Always You (Lexi and Noah)

My Second Chance (Juliette and Easton)

My Mistletoe Mix-Up (Raven and Logan)

Forever Yours (Alyssa and Jace)

**Eden Falls Academy Series:**

The Charade (Ava and Carter)

The Facade (Cambrielle and Mack)

The Ruse (Elyse and Asher)

The Confidant (Scarlett and Hunter)

The Confession (Kiara and Nash)

**Standalone YA**

Protect My Heart (Emma and Arie)

Kissing The Boy Next Door (Lauren and Wes)

**Rich and Famous Series:**

Assisting My Brother's Best Friend (Kate and Drew)

Hollywood and Ivy (Ivy and Justin)

Her Football Star Ex (Emerson and Vincent)

Friend Zone to End Zone (Arianna and Cole)

Stolen Kisses from a Rock Star (Maya and Landon)

# EXCERPT FROM FOREVER YOURS
## JACE

Me: **We're in your backyard now. Logan is about to come in looking like me.**

I shot the text to my friend, Trey, and then turned to look at my identical twin brother, Logan. He wore the same blueish-gray jacket, light blue T-shirt, dark blue jeans and light gray shoes as me—an outfit our mom had given us for our seventeenth birthday last month.

Yes, even though we were juniors in high school, our mom still tried to get us to dress alike.

It came in handy sometimes though. Like on nights like tonight when we wanted to test our old friends and see just how well they could tell us apart after eighteen months away.

Logan straightened his shoulders. "Should I head in to the party?"

"Just a sec," I said, checking to make sure he didn't have a hair out of place. We couldn't have his "run a hand through his hair and call it good" style showing through and giving us away.

As identical twins, there weren't a lot of ways that we could set ourselves apart from one another, so years ago Logan had started wearing his hair slightly longer than me and went for what I'd heard lots of girls call his "hot, bad-boy look."

I had chosen to go to the opposite end of the spectrum and opted for the clean-cut and trendy look. I'd even gone through a short phase where I'd worn fake glasses just because I hated getting in trouble for things Logan did.

Thankfully I'd realized what a dork I was and had ditched the glasses a couple of years ago.

But since we were going all-out with tonight's switcheroo, Logan had allowed me to drag him to the barber shop last week before we moved back to Ridgewater, and we'd both gotten the same haircut.

Logan had only complained a little.

"Does my hair meet your anal-retentive standards?" Logan asked, noticing my inspection.

I took in his brown hair. He had used the pomade I'd let him borrow, styling his hair just like I always did. And he'd even taken the time to tame the cowlick at the back of his head.

Deciding he did look just like me, I nodded and said, "I don't think anyone will tell the difference, unless they're paying close attention to your mannerisms. In fact, I doubt mom or dad could even tell us apart."

"Good." He grinned. "And if someone figures it out, I guess we'll know they're our true friend."

I laughed. "I guess it's good I already told Trey about the switch then. Can't have him disappointing me on our first night back."

Speaking of the devil, my phone buzzed with a text.

Trey: **Perfect. Send Logan in.**

Logan grabbed his water bottle—something that would only deepen everyone's assumptions that he was indeed Jace Carmichael at the party instead of Logan, since they didn't know that he'd gotten sober last year.

"I'm gonna head in," Logan said. "I'll make the rounds and then come back to make the switch in about twenty minutes. Try not to freeze while you're out here."

I watched my brother walk up the steps to Trey's upper deck and zipped up my coat to ward off the cold. It probably would've been smart to have chosen to be the one inside the warm house, pretending to be the other, given that it was December in New York and I was still used to the nicer temperatures of North Carolina. But, when deciding who would go inside first, I couldn't pass up the opportunity to let him make the first contact with a certain person whom I wasn't sure how to greet.

If Logan could make that first meeting less awkward for me, then standing out in the cold for twenty minutes would be well worth it.

It had been eighteen months since I'd let Alyssa Turner see through my usually confident exterior and fumble my way through my first kiss ever. Eighteen months for me to cringe every time I thought about that kiss and how nervous I'd probably seemed to her. Eighteen months for me to wonder if she'd only let me kiss her because she felt bad saying no to me on my last night in Ridgewater.

I hadn't always thought the kiss had gone badly; I'd actually been on cloud nine for the first few weeks after it. But when Alyssa started dating my best friend Trey shortly after, I realized that the kiss I'd relived so many times and daydreamed about had probably just been a pity kiss on her end.

I cringed again. I'd been such a fool to think a last-minute kiss would be a grand romantic gesture.

Oh well. Time had passed, and I'd dated a few girls and kissed several others while we'd lived in Sweet Water. So if Alyssa had told any of her friends about what a bad kisser I was, I could now demonstrate a much higher level of expertise and make it look like she was simply remembering that summer night incorrectly.

But even though I was much more confident in my abilities to kiss a girl the right way, that didn't mean I wasn't still anxious about seeing Alyssa for the first time.

I'd practically bared my soul to her that night by telling her I'd been in love with her since elementary. So if Logan could go in there, talk to Alyssa and let her assume he was a new, more confident me, then that would be great. Logan had never crushed on her and therefore wouldn't have any sort of reaction that I was worried I might have.

And then once that initial meeting was over with, I could go to the party and pretend like everything was normal. We wouldn't have to even address that stupid lapse in judgment, and she could continue dating Trey without feeling bad for me.

---

I was just about to text Logan and tell him I was freezing outside, and that he needed to get his butt out here, when a text from him came through on my phone.

Logan: **I've talked to pretty much everyone at the party. They all bought it.**

I didn't know how to feel about that. Should I be sad that none of my friends had seen through Logan's disguise?

Then an even more disturbing thought came to mind. If no one had noticed anything was off, it meant that even Alyssa hadn't been able to tell the difference between Logan and me.

Despite my embarrassing kiss, I had still always felt so *seen* by her. She had never once been fooled by me and my twin's shenanigans. She'd always been able to tell when we were pretending to be the other.

I'd always just been Jace Carmichael with Alyssa. Not *'I'm pretty sure he's Jace, but he could also be Logan.'*

My shoulders drooped with the thought. I guess it made sense though. She hadn't seen us in a year-and-a-half.

But I had to text Logan just to make sure she had fallen for the trick too and that he had actually talked to her and cleared everything up.

Me: **Did Alyssa not pick up on the switch then?**

Logan: **She isn't at the party.**

What?

A mixture of relief and disappointment passed through me.

Me: **Why isn't she at the party?**

It was Trey's party. Why wouldn't Alyssa be at her boyfriend's party?

*Unless they had broken up...*

I immediately squashed down the hope that surfaced with that thought. I would not be the guy who waited around for his best friend to break up with his girlfriend just so I could have a second chance at kissing her the right way this time.

My phone vibrated, bringing me back to the present.

Logan: **I asked a few of the girls on the cheer team whether Raven and Alyssa were coming and they said that they thought so. Apparently Raven embarrassed herself at the basketball game and needed a pep talk from Alyssa before they came.**

The tightness in my chest relaxed. She was still coming.

But then the disappointment soon followed. If she was still coming, that meant she was still with Trey.

Man, I needed to get my crap together. My emotions were all over the place tonight.

Which meant that I really needed Logan to be the one to break the ice for me. I would rather freeze out here than be inside for that initial meeting.

So I shot Logan another message.

Me: **Give them another 5 minutes. I know how much you wanted to see Raven.**

Logan: **More like I know how much you don't want to get caught staring at Alyssa when her boyfriend is watching.**

I shoved my phone into my pocket, deciding not to even respond to that. That was the fun thing about being a twin. It was hard to keep secrets.

I stuffed my hands into my coat pockets and paced around the small rectangle of cement that had been protected from the snow by the deck above. A few minutes later, I heard the back door open and the sound of footsteps on the wood planks.

Good. Logan must have talked to Alyssa and Raven already.

I was just about to make my way up the stairs to meet him when I heard another set of footsteps step outside before the door shut.

Had he brought someone with him?

I guess it shouldn't surprise me since Logan had never had much difficulty in getting a girl to like him.

The Carmichael twins did have a certain charm.

"What's the surprise you have for me, Trey?" a feminine voice asked.

My knee's buckled when I recognized it, and I had to lean against the house for support.

*Oh, crap!*

Trey was bringing Alyssa to see me.

My face flushed with heat. I needed to get out of here. I wasn't ready to face her yet. Logan needed to take away the awkwardness first.

Trey's voice sounded next. "Just a minute and you can see my surprise for yourself."

And before I could figure out my escape route, their footsteps sounded on the steps.

Ten seconds later, she came into view. And when our eyes met, she looked like she'd just seen a ghost.

"Jace?" she gasped, shaking her head like she wasn't quite sure she was actually seeing me. "I-is that really you?"

And in those few seconds, I realized she was even more beautiful than I'd remembered. Her honey-colored, blonde hair framed her face in soft curls. Her cheeks were slightly pink from the cold night air. And her eyes were just as bright blue as I'd remembered.

"Yeah, it's me." I managed to smile, though my pulse was racing so hard I could hear it in my ears.

*Just act cool, Jace. Let her see the confident version of you—the version that had always been able to flirt with any girl, no matter how out of his league she was.*

*Don't revert back to the fifteen-year-old guy who was*

*shaking the whole time he was confessing his feelings to his long-time crush.*

I'd always prided myself on my ability to talk to anyone and everyone. I'd never had trouble striking up a conversation or flirting with a pretty girl. But things were different with Alyssa.

Alyssa was just so good. An amazing person through and through.

That's why I'd been so elated when she'd kissed me back. I'd actually gotten the girl.

Well, until Trey swooped in and stole her.

"Is this my surprise?" She looked to Trey with a question in her eyes. "Jace is my surprise?"

"Yes." Trey smiled, his typical happy-go-lucky-grin. "Isn't it the best surprise?"

Alyssa looked back to me, her lips parted like she still wasn't sure she believed that I was here.

I held my breath as I waited for her to say what she thought about seeing me again. Was she happy? Disappointed? Or just neutral about the whole thing?

I'd tried to imagine this moment so many times but had never been able to decide how I thought she would react.

After a few heart-pounding moments, her soft pink lips turned up into a smile and she said, "This is the best surprise."

*The best surprise.*

Should I be interpreting that?

Before I could figure out exactly what she had meant, she released Trey's hand and stepped closer to me. She hugged me and whispered something that sounded like, "I've missed you so much."

My heart thumped hard in my chest.

I really wanted to interpret her words as meaning that she hadn't kissed me out of pity back then. That she too might have liked me, at least a little.

I barely had time to return the hug and catch a whiff of her light perfume before she stepped away again, leaving me colder than I'd been before.

And when our eyes met again, there was a torn expression in them that I didn't understand.

Trey stepped forward next to give me a hug, breaking the eye contact Alyssa and I had been sharing.

"It's so good to have you back, Jace," he said, patting me on the back.

"It's great to be back."

"Wait?" Alyssa asked when Trey returned to his spot by her side. "Are you like, back, back? Or just visiting?"

"My family just moved back to Ridgewater." I pushed my hands into my pockets. "So I'm back, back."

The flash of excitement in her eyes made my heart stutter in my chest.

I cleared my throat. "So, Trey tells me that you two are dating."

"Yes." She nodded and stepped closer to him as if just remembering. "We are."

"You might say I'm one lucky dog." Trey put his arm around Alyssa's shoulders and gave her a quick kiss on the cheek before saying, "So do you think we should get you inside and introduce the real you to everyone?"

Alyssa narrowed her eyes. "Did you and Logan switch places again?"

A guilty smile lifted my lips. "Maybe."

She shook her head and laughed. "You guys haven't changed a bit, have you?"

"Not too much, I guess."

And the smile she gave me then lit up her whole face. She'd always been breathtaking when she smiled like that.

I'd missed her more than I thought.

"I, um, guess we should probably get you back in the house and warmed up, huh?" She tucked a lock of hair behind her ear like she was suddenly self-conscious. "I bet there are a lot of people who will be excited to see you—the real you, that is."

I nodded. "Let's hope so, at least."

I gestured for them to lead the way, and when Trey reached for Alyssa's hand, I tried not to notice the way it made my stomach twist in a knot.

Watching them be boyfriend and girlfriend was going to be an interesting experience.

Hopefully it wouldn't be painful as well.

## CHAPTER TWO
### ALYSSA

"So how was it coming back to winter?" I asked Jace over my shoulder as we walked up the steps to Trey's back door, my heart still pounding from the past few minutes.

I still couldn't believe that he was back. I'd been sure Trey had brought me outside to give me an early Christmas present. I'd never thought in a million years that Jace Carmichael would be back there.

I never thought I'd see him again.

"It's a lot colder than Sweet Water," Jace answered, his voice deeper that I remembered. "But I'm looking forward to having fun in all of the snow this year."

His voice wasn't the only thing that was different about him. He was a few inches taller than he'd been at the end of our freshman year. His shoulders were broader.

His jaw more defined, though he still had the dimples I'd always loved.

Yes, Jace Carmichael had somehow gotten even better looking in the last year-and-a-half.

I pushed that thought away. I wasn't supposed to notice things like that. Especially not while holding the hand of my boyfriend.

"So when we go inside, should I introduce you to all the girls as available, or are you still dating that girl you were dating last summer?" Trey asked when we all made it to the upper deck.

"Oh, um..." Jace pushed his hands in his pockets, his eyes darting to mine briefly. "I'm not dating anyone right now."

He'd been dating someone?

Of course he'd been dating someone. It would be stranger if he hadn't. He was Jace. He'd probably dated all kinds of girls in the past year-and-a-half.

What had his girlfriends been like?

Before I could wonder if they'd been prettier than me, I pushed those thoughts away.

I shouldn't care that he'd dated anyone while he'd been gone. I certainly hadn't just sat around and waited for him to come back.

*We hadn't thought he was coming back.*

## CHAPTER TWO

"Is something wrong?" Trey touched my shoulder, bringing me back to the present.

"Oh." I focused my gaze on his face. "Yeah, sorry. I was just thinking about something."

Trey narrowed his eyes at me, inspecting my face. But instead of pressing me further, he shrugged and said, "Okay."

Then he led the way to the back door of his house and pushed it open.

There was a shuffling of footsteps as my friend, Raven, and Jace's twin, Logan, quickly moved out of the way of the door.

"Oh, hi, guys," I said as we stepped inside Trey's kitchen, happy they were right here and we didn't have to go looking for them.

"Hi," Raven responded, a confused expression on her face as she looked from the twin beside her to the twin who had come in right behind me.

"We were just coming to show you my surprise," Trey said to Raven. "But it looks like you already figured it out."

"Yeah," Raven said, her cheeks pinker than usual. "Jace and I were just reacquainting ourselves with one another."

I furrowed my brow and pointed to the twin behind me. "But this is Jace."

Apparently Logan had done a great job at pretending to be his brother, because Raven had crushed on Jace just like I had growing up and should have known the difference.

Would I have been able to tell the difference if they'd tried their trick on me?

I hoped so. Jace had told me once that I was the only person they could never trick. I didn't want to lose that talent.

"Hi, Raven." Jace waved, his arm brushing against mine with the movement. "Long time, no see."

"Hi...?" Raven turned back to the Carmichael twin she'd already been talking to. "Logan?"

Logan smirked and shook his head. "It was a pleasure to run into you again, Raven."

The look on Raven's face confirmed that she had indeed thought she had been talking to Jace before we'd come in. And Logan's smile grew even bigger.

He leaned in to whisper something in her ear. I couldn't pick out what he said, but the annoyed look on Raven's face told me it wasn't something she wanted to hear.

Then Logan leaned back and spoke louder, "It was great to see you all again. But if you'll excuse me, I have somewhere else to be."

And instead of sticking around to chat, he opened the back door and left the party.

## CHAPTER TWO

"Logan didn't feel like staying?" I turned back to Jace.

"Logan had only planned to be here for a few minutes. He tries to avoid the party scene these days," Jace said.

I nodded. Logan had always been the first one to suggest we raid their parents' wine cabinet back in the day. But I'd noticed he had been holding a water bottle today. Maybe he had decided to take the same approach as Jace and was staying away from alcohol now.

"Good for him," I said.

"Hey, Jace," Trey said from the other side of me. "Want me to take you around to introduce you to everyone?"

"Sure." Jace gave me a quick look before sliding his gaze to Trey. "We should probably clear up whatever confusion Logan caused while I was freezing outside."

Trey gave me a quick kiss on the cheek. "Be back in a bit, babe," he said. Then he and Jace headed into the living room where most of the basketball team and cheerleaders were celebrating tonight's win.

Once the boys were out of sight, Raven turned to me. "So what were you all doing outside while I was getting tricked by Logan?"

I took off my coat and hung it on the coat tree by the door. "Trey was just excited to have Jace back in town and wanted to surprise me. We didn't really do anything besides talk."

"And how is Jace?" Raven raised an eyebrow and stepped closer. "Does he seem the same?"

I shrugged. "We didn't really have time to dig into everything, but he seemed like the same guy to me."

"Same guy, but somehow even hotter." Raven looked toward the living room as if hoping for another glimpse of Jace. But he and Trey had already gone to a different part of the house that we couldn't see. "I mean, he looks hotter to you too, right?"

I pressed my lips together as I tried to decide how to answer that. Normally I was fine talking with Raven about how good-looking a particular guy was, but talking about Jace like that was different. We had both crushed on him, and now that I was dating Trey, me saying something about how attractive Jace had turned out to be might make it seem like I was being unfaithful to my boyfriend.

But then again, not talking about it would probably make it look like I had something to hide.

And I didn't.

So I said, "Yes, Jace and Logan both turned out alright."

Raven scrunched up her nose and crossed her arms. "I don't want to talk about Logan."

"Why?"

"Just because." She shrugged and took a sip of her water—like she was trying really hard to seem bored with the conversation.

"Raven...?" I prodded. "What happened with you and Logan while I was outside?"

"Nothing." Her voice came out higher-pitched than usual.

I smiled at my friend. "The guilty look on your face makes me think that it wasn't just nothing."

She drew in a deep breath and sighed. "Fine. But promise you won't be mad at me."

I frowned. Why would I be mad about what she and Logan had talked about?

Unless Logan had told her about me and Jace kissing...

My skin prickled with the thought.

Logan better not have told her. Raven had already had a bad enough time at the basketball game. Tonight would not be the right time for her to find out that Jace had picked me instead of her.

I swallowed. "Just tell me."

Her shoulders relaxed and she sighed. "So you remember how we had that pact since eighth grade where we said that since we both really liked Jace, we'd let Jace choose who he liked most out of the two of us?"

"Yes..." I said the word slowly, a jumble of nerves wiggling their way into my stomach.

Had Logan really told her?

If I'd known the Carmichael twins were moving back to Ridgewater, I would have found a way to tell Raven that Jace had already picked me. But since I hadn't known, I'd figured it was probably best to just keep that to myself.

It shouldn't have been an issue.

Except that they moved back and stupid Logan had probably thought that Raven already knew about it.

"Well," Raven continued, giving me an apologetic look. "I figured that since you were dating Trey now, that it would probably be okay for me to stop waiting for Jace to decide between the two of us."

"What do you mean?" I asked, my face flushing with heat. Did this mean that Logan hadn't told her, then?

She looked down at the cup she was holding before meeting my gaze again. "I, um, I kind of already kissed Jace tonight."

"What?" I said the word loudly as my heart thudded against my ribcage. "What do you mean, you kissed Jace?"

How was that possible?

We'd gotten to the party at the same time.

"Well, not Jace-Jace obviously," she hurried to say.

"But I thought Logan was Jace and so I ended up kissing him under the mistletoe right before you guys came in."

"Oh." Relief rushed through me. "So you and *Logan* kissed?" That was so much different.

*So* much different.

"Yes." She covered her eyes with her hand briefly, like she was embarrassed.

"And how was it?" I smiled. I couldn't care less if she'd kissed Logan.

She uncovered her eyes and looked at me guiltily. "It was pretty amazing, actually." She shook her head. "But that doesn't matter, because I'd been under the impression that it was Jace and not Logan. If I'd known I was actually kissing Logan, I'm sure I would have hated the kiss."

Sure, she would have.

I knew the Carmichael twins well. And while I had always gravitated more towards Jace's personality, there were plenty of girls at our school who were going to go wild once they knew that bad boy Logan Carmichael was back.

"That Logan always was smooth," I teased.

"Can we just try to forget about Logan and get back to Jace?" She shook her head. "What I'm wanting to know is whether you're okay with me going after Jace now."

"Oh."

"Are you mad?" She scrunched up her face. "Do you want me to stay away?"

"No, I'm not mad," I said.

Slightly threatened...?

A tad bit jealous....?

Maybe.

Raven must have picked up on my vibes because she said, "I totally get it if you want me to find someone else. We had just made that pact so long ago, and with our circumstances being different now, I figured it might be okay."

I forced my expression to remain unbothered. "No, that's fine. I'm dating Trey now, so of course you should be free to go after Jace if you want to."

"Really?"

"Of course," I said. "I mean, it would be perfect for you and Jace to date since he and Trey are best friends and me and you are best friends. We could all hang out all the time."

Raven practically beamed at me and then gave me a hug. "That would be so amazing. Now I just need to get myself on Jace's radar again and hope Logan doesn't interfere next time."

Read what happens next in FOREVER YOURS.

# ABOUT THE AUTHOR

Judy Corry is the USA Today Bestselling Author of YA and Contemporary Romance. She writes romance because she can't get enough of the feeling of falling in love. She's known for writing heart-pounding kisses, endearing characters, and hard-won happily ever afters.

She lives in Southern Utah with the boy who took her to Prom, their four amazing kids, two dogs and a cate. She's addicted to love stories, dark chocolate and chai lattes.

Made in the USA
Monee, IL
03 May 2024